Secrets Among The Stones

The Pineworth Chronicles, Volume 4

K.E.W.

Published by White Quill Writings, 2024.

SECRETS AMONG THE STONES

First edition. March 18, 2024.

ISBN: 979-8224024582

Written by K.E.W..

Also by K.E.W.

The Pineworth Chronicles
The Crossroads Of Duty
The Often Forgotten Hero
A Rookie's Journey
Secrets Among The Stones

Standalone
The Pineworth Chronicles

Table of Contents

To my parents,

Your love has been my compass, guiding me through the uncharted territories of life. Your sacrifices have built the foundation upon which I stand today. Your unwavering support has been a source of strength and inspiration in moments of joy and sorrow.

This book is a testament to the values, resilience, and boundless love you've instilled in me. Thank you for fostering my dreams, encouraging my pursuits, and being the silent heroes behind the scenes.

With love and gratitude, K.E.W.

Prologue

The quiet town of Pineworth, Georgia. A place with small-town people and small-town politics is about to be confronted with an ugly truth.

For nearly two centuries, the citizens of the quaint city had been taught to believe their city was one of great history that had always promoted a sense of equal opportunity.

The facade of charm has masked a web of unmentioned lies, betrayal, and unresolved grievances.

Dark secrets will be exposed. Prominent people will be involved.

A detective will be pushed to his limits in a quest for answers. He will have to delve deep into Pineworth for unknown answers and clues.

After cutting his teeth on the beat, Alex Bennett has been a Detective for the Pineworth police department for some time now. He has made this job his life. Will he be able to shoulder the load of such a case?

Will the lone wolf detective be able to take help and advice from co-workers?

This will be the test of a lifetime for Alex and his town.

The stage is set for a gripping journey through the heart and soul of a town fighting with its own identity.

Chapter 1
A Grave Discovery

Rays of sunshine spilled over the horizon, emitting beautiful rays upon Pineworth's ancient cemetery. They danced gracefully between the tombstones, casting an ever-enchanting aura over the grounds.

However, the scene that was usually a place of peace and remembrance is suddenly shattered by the bright lights and alarming sirens of the local police cars, calling Detective Alex Bennett into the heart of a new mystery. The air was thick, saturated with the scent of freshly dug earth combined with personal floral notes.

The difference between the usual atmosphere and the unfolding tragedy was obvious. Among the pristine gravesites, the lifeless body of Henry Winters lay in a haunting stillness.

His rugged face exuded a sense of history, now frozen forever in an eternal slumber. There was a straightforward narrative etched in the scene—the peaceful gravesites were disrupted by violent chaos and the telltale signs of a brutal struggle.

The vibrant hues of floral arrangements juxtaposed against the scattered petals, remnants of a battle that changed the discord within this sacred ground.

The torn ribbons and overturned vases hinted at a battle fought between love and loss, leaving behind a haunting reminder of the pain and turmoil that had transpired in this hallowed place.

Still clutching an ancient journal, Henry Winters' hand told a tale of desperation—a valiant effort to preserve a secret, protect a legacy, or unravel the truth before his untimely demise.

As Alex knelt beside the victim, the moment's weight settled upon him. The look of betrayal and brutality stained the very core of this scene, and it spoke volumes. This wasn't merely a murder; it was a betrayal of trust, a violation of the sanctity of a town known for its peaceful demeanor.

With each passing moment, he felt the urgency to uncover the truth. The whispers of secrets buried within the weathered pages of the journal resonated through the cemetery, promising answers that could shed light on this heinous act.

Determined lines etched themselves upon his face—a resolve to seek justice for Henry Winters and to untangle the web of lies that had darkened the town's legacy. As the morning light danced upon the gravestones, Alex vowed to pursue the truth, knowing that the memory of this betrayal would resonate until justice prevailed.

Bennett approached Officer Nathan Reynolds, who stood near the crime scene's perimeter, expressing concern and solemnity.

Alex cleared his throat, his voice calm yet authoritative amidst the chaos. "Officer Reynolds, I need your account of what you found."

Still coming to terms with the gravity of the situation, Nathan nodded, his gaze fixed on the crime scene. "I was on patrol when I received a call over the radio about a possible disturbance here at the cemetery. When I got here, I noticed this area had been disturbed. That's when I found Mr. Winters." His tone was measured, betraying the magnitude of the discovery.

"Did you notice anything peculiar when you arrived?" Alex probed gently, sensing the weight on Nathan's shoulders.

Nathan hesitated momentarily before responding, "There was an eerie quietness. No one else was around. It was as if this dreadful incident unfolded silently." His voice trailed off as he glanced back at the crime scene, a mix of frustration and determination evident in his eyes.

Alex touched Nathan's shoulder, noticing the young officer's hard time with what he had just seen. "You did well to secure the area, Officer. Thank you. Now, I need you to retrace your steps. Anything, no matter how small, could be crucial."

Nathan nodded, steeling himself for the recount. "I approached cautiously. The graves nearby seemed disturbed, and there were signs of a struggle—torn foliage and upturned soil. That's when I found Mr. Winters, his hand gripping that old journal." He gestured towards the journal, a key piece of the puzzle.

"Good work, Officer," Alex advises, his gaze shifting back to the scene. "This case is going to demand our best. I'll need your vigilance and attention to detail."

Nathan nodded, a determined resolve settling in. "Absolutely, Detective. I'm here to help in any way I can."

As Alex and Nathan continued their conversation, the weight of the investigation hung heavy in the air, both men knowing that Nathan's details could be crucial in unraveling the secrets buried within the cemetery.

Alex knew the kind of attention this case would get. This man was great in the community. He was someone that everyone knew. A pillar in the community for a very long time.

"Who would do this?" he thought to himself.

Alex stood beside the lifeless body of Henry Winters; his brows furrowed in concentration.

Detective Maya Sinclair is a seasoned investigator known for her keen eye and astute observations.

Maya examined the body, her experienced gaze scanning for clues, and walked up beside Alex.

Alex gives her a look as if to see what she is doing. He wasn't known to enlist the help of the other detectives. He always liked the fact that he could solve a case on his own.

"The cause of death seems to be blunt force trauma," she remarked, gesturing towards the injuries on Henry's head. "The blows were forceful, indicating a struggle before his demise."

Alex nodded, agreeing with Maya's assessment. He knew she was right.

"It aligns with the signs of a struggle we found around the gravesite." He then turned his attention to the aged journal still tightly clutched in Henry's hand.

As Alex carefully pried open the journal, Maya leaned in, her interest piqued. "What have you found?"

"A missing page," Alex replied, pointing to the void within the journal. "It's not just missing; it looks like someone might have intentionally torn out the page."

Was the page a reason for the murder? Or just a casualty in the crime?

Maya's raised an eyebrow. "That suggests someone didn't want certain information getting out. There could be crucial details in that torn-out section."

"Absolutely," Alex agreed. "The missing page might be the link to understanding Henry and why he was murdered."

Together, they meticulously cataloged the evidence, including the torn-out page, understanding its significance. The missing section within the journal seemed to hold the secrets Henry had unearthed, secrets someone was desperate to conceal.

As they continued their analysis, the torn-out page remained a focal point—a piece of the puzzle that could unravel the mystery behind Henry Winters' untimely death.

Alex and Maya exchanged a determined glance, their shared resolve evident. Unraveling the truth hidden within the journal was crucial to solving the enigmatic murder that had shaken the tranquility of Pineworth.

As the day was unfolding Alex could start seeing that having Detective Sinclair there was a tool for him. He had never had the experience of bouncing ideas off someone else while on scene. Not since his days as a beat cop.

Alex searched the area surrounding Henry Winters' body, looking for any trace of a murder weapon. With a lot of care, he carefully went through the soil and examined the nearby gravestones, hoping for a clue that might explain the violent act that had altered the cemetery's peace.

Despite his thorough search, the landscape yielded no tangible evidence of the murder weapon. The lack of a physical object sent ripples of frustration through Alex's mind, a puzzle missing a crucial piece.

He knelt beside the lifeless body, reexamining the immediate area for any overlooked detail. His gloved hands traced the ground, fingers sifting through the soil in a desperate attempt to uncover something—anything—that might serve as a lead.

"No murder weapon," he muttered under his breath, letting a hint of frustration show.

Detective Maya joined his search, her trained eyes scanning the area alongside his. "Nothing here either," she commented, sharing in Alex's dismay.

"It's not like the murder weapon can vanish," Alex murmured, his mind racing through the possibilities. The absence of a murder weapon added another layer of complexity to an ever-growing case.

As they continued looking for anything they could use, a sense of unease settled over Alex. The absence of a tangible clue weighed on him heavily; the loss of a murder weapon cast a dark cloud over the investigation. It was a reminder that sometimes, the most crucial clues lay hidden and unseen.

A sudden commotion caught his attention as Alex continued his forensic examination of the crime scene. From the corner of his eye, he spotted Henry Winters' distraught son and wife rushing toward the area, and their faces were that of shock and grief.

Reacting swiftly, Alex motioned to the nearby officers. "Hold them back. Keep them from the crime scene," he instructed the officers, understanding the delicacy of the situation. He wanted to shield the family from the distressing sight of Henry's body and, at the same time, protect a crime scene that was already proving to be fragile.

The officers responded quickly to his orders, intercepting the son and wife before they reached the area of the crime scene. Despite their heartfelt pleas and saddened cries, the officers held firm but gently guided them away from the area, trying to offer them a safe place to mourn in a time of grief.

Alex watched from a distance, and he was torn between the urgency of the investigation and the empathy he felt for the grieving family. He knew the importance of preserving the integrity of the crime scene and also shielding the family from the distressing sight of Henry's body in its current state.

He understood they must be in immense pain after experiencing the loss of a father and husband.

But he also knew that at this moment, the priority was to maintain the sanctity of the investigation and protect the family from the ugly scene while hopefully shielding them from the painful sight. Hopefully, this will allow them to retain their cherished memories of Henry Winters untouched by the horrifying reality of his demise.

Alex, who couldn't help but see the anguish across Henry Winters' wife and son, approached them with a sad yet gentle demeanor. While taking measured steps, he offered condolences and wanted to reassure them in their time of distress.

"Mrs. Winters, I'm Detective Alex Bennett," he began, hoping his voice was a mix of empathy and professionalism. "I'm deeply sorry for your loss. I assure you and your son that we are doing everything possible to uncover the truth surrounding Henry's passing."

Tears formulated in Mrs. Winters' eyes as she looked up at Alex, her voice shaking with emotion. "He didn't deserve this. He was a good man," she whispered, her grief showing in her voice and face.

Alex nodded to show his understanding, a sympathetic expression on his face. "I want to assure you, we will work tirelessly to find out what happened," he reiterates to her, showing the determination behind his intent.

Turning to Henry's son Matthew, Alex touched his shoulder. "I know this is incredibly difficult, but we're committed to finding answers. Your father meant a lot to this town; we owe it to him and your family to seek justice."

Matthew was in a state of shock, standing still, his eyes with a look of sorrow and disbelief.

"If there's anything you need or anything you remember that might help us, please don't hesitate to reach out," Alex offered gently, his tone conveying to them that he meant what he was saying.

After the grieving family nodded in appreciation, Alex stepped back, wanting to allow them a moment of privacy in a time of ever-changing emotions.

As Alex stepped away from the Winters family, a renewed sense of determination settled within him. He then redirected his attention back to the crime scene, urging himself and his team to intensify their efforts.

The sun cast stretched shadows across the cemetery, highlighting the calmness that sharply contrasted with the turmoil surrounding the murder. Alex's eyes scanned the ground, and he called over the forensic team, pointing out a disturbed area very near to Henry's body.

"Let's put some focus on the soil," he directed, gesturing toward the scattered artifacts and flower fragments nearby. "Collect every fragment you can, every trace. We need to analyze them all."

The forensic experts diligently began their work, carefully bagging the fragments of flowers, soil samples, and scattered artifacts. As they worked, Alex crouched beside the disarrayed gravestones, noting the disturbance and a few sets of footprint impressions.

"Take detailed photographs of these gravestones and footprint impressions," he instructed, recognizing the potential significance of the disrupted markers.

His keen eyes also caught sight of faint traces of blood near the victim's body. "Blood traces here," he muttered to Maya, who was scrutinizing the scene alongside him. "Seems like the assault might have occurred right at this spot."

Maya nodded in agreement, her eyes scanning the surroundings. "I will help document everything and make sure we do it down to the smallest detail," she affirmed, her determination mirroring Alex's.

As the forensic team continued to collect evidence and document every find, Alex's mind raced with possibilities.

But amid the chaos, a sudden commotion broke the silence of the cemetery. A young woman rushed towards Alex, her breathless voice filled with urgency.

"Detective Bennett! Detective Bennett!" she called out, her eyes widened with apprehension.

Startled by the unexpected interruption, Alex turned his attention to the young woman, and he looked at her with curiosity. "How can I help you?" he asked, his voice steady despite the whirlwind of emotions that was going through him.

The woman continued to gasp for air before speaking again. "I... I think I saw something... something important," she stammered, her voice unable to hold back the mix of fear and excitement.

Alex's interest was piqued. He began by motioning for the woman to calm down and then try to share her information. After gathering herself, she began to recount her encounter that admittedly raised hope within Alex's heart.

"I was out here for a quiet walk just before dusk," she started, her voice filled with the determination to tell her story. "I was walking through the cemetery, admiring the beautiful tombstones and the peaceful atmosphere. But as I passed by the old oak tree over there, I saw a man in the shadows."

Alex leaned forward, making sure his focus was solely on the young woman as she continued her account. "What did this man look like?" he pressed, eager to gather any details that could potentially lead them closer to some answers.

"I can tell he was tall, and from where I was, he had a menacing presence," she replied, her voice quivering slightly. "His face was blocked from view by a hat pulled really low past his eyebrows, but I distinctly remember his eyes. They were cold, like ice."

Maya, standing next to Alex, scribbled down notes as fast as she could, trying to capture every word of the woman's description. Alex nodded, urging her to continue.

"I didn't want to get too close or be seen, so I stayed hidden behind a large tombstone," she continued.

"That is all I saw, though," she said. "As soon as I came from behind the tombstone, he was gone."

Alex's mind began to race with possibilities.

Could this mysterious man be the answer to unraveling the truth behind Henry Winters' murder? Alex couldn't help but feel a sense of hope surging within him. Especially after the crime scene itself was giving them nothing.

He thanked the woman for coming forward, doing his best to express his gratitude for her bravery and willingness to share her encounter.

"Your information could prove to be invaluable," he said sincerely, his voice filled with appreciation and also a little anticipation. "We will do everything we can to investigate this lead further."

As Alex turned to relay the woman's account to the officers on the scene, he noticed the Winters family standing at a distance, their eyes fixed on him. Their faces show grief and desperation, both longing for justice to be served. Alex approached them, his steps gentle yet with a show of determination.

"I wanted to let you know I just spoke with a witness who saw something suspicious near the crime scene," he informed them, his voice laced with cautious optimism. "I am going to follow this lead and explore every avenue it may open up."

Alex then took a deep breath as he surveyed the now-empty crime scene. The police had finished collecting evidence, and the coroner had removed Henry Winters' body not long after, leaving behind nothing but trampled grass and the ever-constant unanswered questions.

As dusk began to fall, a hush seemed to settle over the cemetery. The last rays of sunlight filtered through the trees, casting shadows that stretched across the grounds. Alex stood alone near the old oak tree, the very spot the witness had described seeing the mysterious person lurking.

He tried to picture how the scene would have looked hours earlier - the witness hid behind a tombstone, watching the shadowy figure with icy eyes. What secrets might he have been harboring? Alex wanted to uncover the truth that was hidden within the stranger's sinister presence.

A cold breeze rustled the leaves atop the old oak tree while sending a chill down Alex's spine. He pulled his coat tighter around himself as a blanket of darkness came down on the scene. One by one, the distant street lights flickered on, piercing through the gloom.

Each clue, each fragment of evidence, had the potential to weave a narrative, bringing them closer to untangling the enigma of Henry Winters' tragic death.

Alex took one last look around the now-empty cemetery as darkness enveloped the grounds. He made his way along the winding path back towards the front gates, the beam from his flashlight cutting through the blackness like a knife through butter.

The witness's account was constantly replayed in his mind; her description of the lurking man with icy eyes was locking itself into his memory. Alex couldn't shake the feeling that this mysterious figure held vital clues; his presence seemed too sinister and too near the crime scene to be just coincidental.

As Alex approached the gates, he saw a lone figure emerging from the shadows - Chief Brown. Alex quickened his pace, eagerly wanting to update the Chief on this promising new lead.

"Evening, Alex," Chief Brown greeted as Alex reached him. "No breaks in the case yet, I presume?"

"Well, possibly one," Alex replied. "A witness came forward reporting a suspicious man near the crime scene around the estimated time of death."

Alex then recounted the young woman's chilling depiction of the man - his menacing presence, obscured face, and penetrating icy eyes. Chief Brown showed barely any emotion as he listened intently, stroking his chin as if in contemplation.

"This certainly warrants a close investigation," Chief Brown finally said. "We need to track this guy down, and it could be key to finding out what happened."

Alex nodded. "Whoever he is, he didn't belong there. I hope we're on a path that shows us what really happened to Henry."

Then, a look of sadness flashed across Chief Brown's face at the mention of Henry.

"You know Henry and I were old school buddies a long time ago?" Brown asked.

"Oh, I didn't know that, sir. I'm sorry for your loss. I promise I will do everything in my power to find out what happened." Alex replies.

" I know you will, Alex. You are a great detective. Honestly, it's one of the best. Keep me updated on the case whenever you can. I'll see you later."

As the conversation ended and Alex watched Chief Brown leave, he couldn't help but feel like a heavy burden had been placed on him.

He could sense that this man would be not only on his mind but on everyone's mind in Pineworth.

He was determined to find the answers to the questions that everyone had, and he was determined to do it quickly. He felt a strong sense of responsibility, and he knew that this case would be a test for him.

As Alex slid behind the wheel of his car, the haunting image of the cemetery crime scene was ever-lasting in his mind. The tiny glow of the streetlights painted the dimly lit streets as he drove home, his thoughts consumed by the enigmatic puzzle that was Henry Winters' murder.

The day's events played out in his mind like a film reel, each fragment of evidence and conversation with the Winters family swirling in his thoughts. The torn-out page from the journal, the scattered artifacts, and the disturbing events that took place at the cemetery whispered mysteries that begged to be unraveled.

Driving through the quiet town, Alex's focus remained fixed on the case. He mulled over the evidence in his head, piecing together fragments of information, searching for connections that might unlock the truth behind the untimely demise of Henry Winters.

The pain of Mrs. Winters' sorrowful voice reverberated in his mind, a reminder of the human toll any investigation carried. It fueled his determination to seek justice, not just for the victim but for the grieving family left behind.

The click of the turn signal broke the silence in the car, signaling his approach to his home. Parking in his driveway, Alex sat for a short moment; the weight of the case was heavy on his mind and heart. He knew that the pursuit of truth often demanded sacrifices, sometimes at the cost of any great personal relationship.

Exiting the car, Alex ascended the porch steps, his mind still thinking of the complexities of the investigation. Unlocking the front door, he stepped inside, greeted by the quiet solitude of his home—a sanctuary that contrasted sharply with the chaos of the day's events.

As he settled in, the investigation continued to come into his thoughts, the crime scene unfolding like a complex riddle waiting to be deciphered. Alex knew that the answers lay hidden amidst the shadows and fragments of possible evidence awaiting to be discovered.

"Was that mysterious figure seen by the witness the killer"?

"Why would someone want to hurt someone that was so known in the community"?

Alex was finally able to lay down and relax. Although the questions never went away in his mind.

Chapter 2
Unveiling Shadows

The morning sun peeked through the blinds, casting gentle rows of light across Alex's bedroom. His eyes awakened, the case almost instantly flooding his thoughts, disrupting the morning's peace.

Rubbing away the drowsiness from his eyes, Alex reached for his phone on the nightstand. The muted glow showed an abundance of missed calls and texts, friendly reminders of the investigation's urgency. His mind immediately gravitated back to the unbelievable events at the cemetery.

Ever determined, Alex swung his legs over the edge of the bed, his thoughts immediately focused on the day ahead. As he got dressed, the threads of the case seemed to wove themselves into the very fabric of his morning routine—coffee forgotten, his mind preoccupied with the questions and uncertainties that surrounded the investigation.

With a quick glance at his notes and the thick case file, Alex set out for Henry Winters' home, a crucial destination on his new quest for answers. The drive provided a brief distraction, the familiar streets of Pineworth passing by in a blur as his thoughts remained constantly on the mysteries of the case.

Arriving at the Winters residence, Alex stepped out of his car, a faint sense of anticipation and sorrow mingling with the morning air. He went up the porch steps, his knuckles connecting gently against the door.

Mrs. Winters, her eyes reflecting the signs of grief, answered the door. Her expression showed signs of apprehension and sorrow. Alex offered a sympathetic smile, hopefully, a gesture of understanding in the face of her distress.

"Mrs. Winters, I hope I'm not intruding at all. I wanted to talk to you about Henry," Alex began gently, his voice carrying a tone of compassion.

"Of course, Detective Bennett, come on in," she replied.

Upon entering the home, Alex couldn't help but feel the sadness. The Winter's home was always the talk of the town. The old plantation house had been in Henry's family since just after the town was created.

Henry was known to invite people over. Even whole classes from the local school came to visit as he talked to them about the history of his magnificent home.

As Alex sat across from Mrs. Winters in her living room, the air was thick with a certain sadness. He tried his best to speak softly, starting off by offering condolences and asking about Henry's hobbies and interests.

"Once again, I am sorry for your loss. I truly am. I'm afraid I have to ask a few questions that I hope will help us in this case." Alex says.

Mrs. Winters Nodded. Holding back tears. Alex could tell by her demeanor that just thinking about him right now must be hard.

Alex leaned slightly forward, his expression showing empathy for the situation. "Mrs. Winters, can you think of anyone who might have wanted to harm Henry recently or at all for that matter? Any disputes or conflicts he might have had?"

Mrs. Winters shook her head almost as fast as the question came out, with a solemn sadness clouding her features. "No, Detective. Henry always seemed to be loved by everyone in town. He was kind-hearted and always helped others whenever he could. I can't fathom anyone wishing him any type of harm."

Alex nodded understandingly, responding to her response. "I understand, Mrs. Winters. We're exploring every angle to try to understand what happened. Any small detail might be helpful. Did Henry ever mention feeling concerned or troubled about anything or anyone to you?"

"He was extremely passionate about his work, his history research," she answered, her voice filled with a mixture of sorrow and uncertainty. "But he never mentioned to me about feeling threatened or worried about anyone."

"MRS. WINTERS, COULD you tell me a bit about Henry's activities and passions?" Alex inquired gently, aiming to understand more about Henry's life.

With a faint smile tinged with sorrow, Mrs. Winters nodded. "Henry was devoted to our town's history. I remember him telling me how he would quit his regular job and devote his time to his history. He would spend hours delving into old books and was always curious about our past. He had this journal he cherished more than anything, filled with notes about the town's heritage and secrets that were passed down," she recounted, her voice showing signs of fondness.

"Did he ever mention anything specific about his research or anything that might have concerned him?" Alex attempted to probe further, hoping to get a clue that could shed light on Henry's recent endeavors and activities.

"He was always mentioning his curiosity about certain historical events. Lately, though, he seemed more into that journal than usual," she continued, her eyes looking down at her feet in concern.

"Thank you, Mrs. Winters, for sharing these moments with me," Alex said with a soft nod, hoping that his gratitude was apparent in his demeanor.

Mrs. Winters offered a slight, appreciative smile. "Thank you for all you are doing to solve this case, detective. Henry deserves justice for what happened to him."

"It's my job, ma'am, and I promise that I will do everything in my power to bring him that justice," Alex assures her, his tone changing to a more determined one. "If there's anything else you can remember, no matter how insignificant or small it may seem, please reach out to me or call the police department."

With a small and gentle pat on her hand, Alex rose from the chair, expressing his heartfelt condolences one more time before leaving. Mrs. Winters watched him depart. Her thoughts were no doubt still on the tragic loss and the hope for answers that the investigation might bring.

As Alex stepped out of the Winters' residence, his thoughts remained shrouded in the enigma of Henry Winters' tragic death. The quiet neighborhood closed around him, the somber atmosphere highlighting the weight of the case.

In the far distance, the distinct markings of a police vehicle caught his eye. Officer James Thompson's cruiser rolled to a halt in front of the Winters house, the familiar figure stepping out with a solemn expression painted on his face.

"Detective," James greeted, his voice flushed with sympathy. "I heard about what happened to Henry. I'm here to check in on Matthew, his son. I was his School Resource Officer at Crestwood Elementary and still keep an eye on him from time to time at the high school."

Alex nodded in understanding, a hint of recognition flashing in his eyes. "James, it's good to see you brother. Matthew's inside with his mom."

The two officers shared a brief moment of understanding before James made his way towards the house. His purpose was clear—to offer some solace to the grieving family and provide reassurance to Matthew.

Inside, Alex observed from a distance as James engaged in a heartfelt conversation with Matthew, offering words of comfort and familiarity. He could sense James' genuine concern for the young boy during the surge of emotions that hung in the air.

The exchange seemed to carry a sense of compassion, an obvious testament to James' dedication beyond his role as an officer—to be a supportive figure and a pillar of strength in moments of distress.

As James bid his farewells to the struggling family by offering support and encouragement to Matthew, Alex really recognized the value of such connections in the community. The unity among officers and the community, the bonds forged through shared experiences, resonated with him profoundly in that moment.

As Officer James Thompson made his way back to his cruiser, he couldn't help but notice Alex still standing outside, deep in thought. Concerned, James approached Alex with a steady stride.

"Everything okay, Alex?" James asked, his eyes reflecting a genuine worry.

Alex looked up, a faint smile appearing on his face. "Yeah, I'm just trying to make sense of it all."

James nodded as he shared the understanding passing between them. "I saw you talking to Matthew. It must mean a lot to have you here for him."

"It's important to offer support, especially in times like these," James replied, appreciating the camaraderie among officers.

James leaned against the cruiser. The two officers were sharing a moment of silence just before James spoke up. "This case bothering you a lot, isn't it, Alex?"

Alex sighed as his gaze fixed on the ground. "Yeah, it's a tough one. Henry was well-liked and very dedicated to the town. I just don't see why someone would want to hurt him. It's like trying to solve a puzzle with all the pieces missing."

James nodded, showing he understood the weight of the investigation. "You know, sometimes those puzzles take time to piece them together. I'm sure you'll figure it out, though."

"I hope so," Alex responded, his gaze distant as he stared into the suddenly unfolding night.

The two officers stood in the quiet of the neighborhood, their shared commitment to seeking justice for Henry Winters binding them in a shared pursuit. In the face of uncertainty, they found strength in their collective dedication to the community.

Alex bid Officer James Thompson a nod and a wave as James prepared to depart, his vehicle's engine strumming softly in the background. James returned the gesture with a knowing smile, a silent but strong recognition passing between them.

"Take care, James," Alex called out, his tone carrying appreciation for the brief moment of solitude they'd shared.

"See you around, Alex," James replied with a wave, a sense of assurance coloring his words as he prepared to leave the neighborhood.

Once James drove off, the evening air filled with the ringing of distant traffic and the calm rustle of leaves. Alex remained at the residence for a moment, absorbing the calm of the night, before making his way to his car.

Unlocking the vehicle, Alex settled into the driver's seat, the familiar scent of leather mixed with the evening breeze. The soft glow of the streetlights cast a different ambiance as he glanced at his phone, noticing a call from Detective Maya.

With a sudden flicker of curiosity, Alex answered the call, bringing the phone to his ear. "Hey, Maya, what's up?"

"Hey, I just wanted to let you know the DNA from the evidence at the cemetery came back," she replied.

"The only DNA that was found on the scene was DNA that belonged to one Henry Winters." she continued.

Alex took a deep breath before responding, "Okay, thank you, Maya."

The call with Detective Maya left Alex with a growing sense of frustration. He leaned back in his car seat, exhaling deeply as he processed the information. The revelation that the only DNA found at the scene belonged to Henry was disheartening.

Turning off the phone, Alex ran a hand through his hair, a surge of frustration coursing through him. The darkness of the night encased him, and the stillness of the street contrasted greatly with the turmoil in his mind.

He just couldn't shake off the feeling that the investigation was at a standstill. The absence of external DNA or evidence indicating someone else's involvement felt like he was hitting a dead end.

Every lead he seemed to pursue seemed to dissipate into thin air, leaving him grasping at shadows.

Resting his head against the now cold car seat, Alex stared blankly through the windshield, his thoughts consumed by the unanswered questions that seemed to have clouded the case. The image of Henry's lifeless form at the cemetery haunted him. It had become a constant reminder of the unresolved mystery.

As Alex pondered the lack of progress, a spark of realization pierced through the fog of uncertainty. The memory of Mrs. Winters' words shot through his mind—the mention of Henry's intense interest in the town's history, particularly its origins.

"The journal," Alex murmured to himself as the epiphany started washing over him. Henry's fascination with the town's historical roots might hold a key—a missing link that could possibly provide a breakthrough in the case.

The insane notion that Henry's research into the town's early history might somehow be connected to the tragedy began to take shape in Alex's mind. Could there be something buried in the annals of the past that could have played a part in Henry's demise?

Armed with a newfound determination, Alex reached for his notebook, flipping through the pages and hurriedly jotting down the newfound lead. He needed to dive deeper into the historical records, reexamine Henry's journal, and uncover any clues that might shed light on the mystery surrounding the murder.

After this, Alex decided to head to the police station. He needed the quiet of his office to rethink his newfound approach to the case.

The police station buzzed with activity as Alex delved into the evidence room, carefully sifting through the case files and examining the collected items from the scene. Amid the many documents and items, his gaze fell upon a large calendar hanging on the wall, displaying the upcoming events in Pineworth.

His eyes narrowed as he focused on a particular entry—an inscription written in black ink that caught his attention: "Bi-Centennial Parade: Tomorrow." The realization hit him like a jolt.

Tomorrow marked a very significant milestone in the town's history, an event that Henry Winters might have deemed important enough to attend himself.

A burst of anticipation swelled within Alex as he pondered the possibilities. Perhaps there lay a clue amidst the celebratory atmosphere—a piece of information or maybe even a connection waiting to be uncovered. It was an opportunity he couldn't afford to miss.

With a sense of purpose, Alex made a quick mental note to attend the parade the next day, sensing that it might hold answers to or, at the very least, provide valuable insights into Henry's research, and this could lead to the possible motives behind his tragic fate.

The whisper of his office's fluorescent lights filled the room as Alex stepped inside, locking the door behind him. The dull glow of his desk lamp illuminated the cluttered workspace, casting skinny shadows against the stacks of case files that lined the shelves.

With a sense of urgency, Alex sank deep into his chair, reaching for a notepad and pen. His mind raced as he jotted down key phrases and clues—scribbles that he hoped could unlock the mystery surrounding Henry Winters' murder.

"Journal—town history—cemetery," he repeated aloud, emphasizing each word as he transcribed his thoughts onto the note paper. The memory of the phone call with Detective Maya replayed in his mind, the revelation of Henry's sole DNA at the crime scene a constant reminder of the case's elusive nature.

As he wrote, Alex's eyes fixed on the list, each word sparking a cascade of associations and possible outcomes. The journal Henry had been studying, the town's deep-seated history, and the significance of the cemetery all seemed to be interconnected—a puzzle waiting to be deciphered.

The weight of the investigation pressed upon him, but Alex remained undeterred. With each stroke of the pen, he pieced together little fragments of information, fueling him to delve deeper into the heart of the matter. Time seemed to slip away as he documented every lead and possible route. The enthusiasm of the investigation seemed to be guiding his hand across the paper.

In the dimly lit office, surrounded by the relics of past cases, Alex forged a roadmap—a web of clues that might hold the key to unraveling the story of Henry's demise.

As Alex sat at his desk, hastily shuffling through case notes, a light knock on the door drew his attention. Looking up, he found Sarah Jones, a familiar face from the police department's dispatch center, standing in the doorway.

"Hey, Sarah, come on in," Alex greeted her, gesturing towards the empty chair across from his desk.

"Thanks, Detective Bennett," Sarah replied with a nod, making her way inside and taking a seat. Her demeanor, at first glance, seemed to be that of concern.

"What can I do for you, Sarah?" Alex asked As he put down his notes, curious about her unexpected visit.

Sarah clasped her hands together. A hint of unease was evident in her voice. "I just wanted to talk to you about the call we received regarding Henry Winters at the park the day he was found," she began.

Alex sat up slightly more in his chair, showing his interest. "Sure, go ahead," he encouraged her to continue.

"I was the one who took that call," Sarah admitted, her head down, looking at her hands as she spoke.

"The person who reported it was a man. He didn't give his name and was quite blunt with his answers."

Alex listened attentively, his interest piqued by this new piece of information. "What did he say on the call?"

"He mentioned seeing someone in the park who looked hurt, lying on the ground," Sarah recalled, her memory focused on the details of the call. "But he didn't provide any further information, no descriptions or specifics."

"Did he seem to be hesitant to call or hesitant to talk?" Alex inquired, trying to figure out the caller's demeanor.

"He seemed like he was trying to be direct, almost too much, but he didn't seem hesitant per se," Sarah explained, trying to recall the details of the conversation. "It was more like he was in a hurry to say what he saw and then to be off the line as soon as possible."

Alex nodded, processing the information. "Thanks for letting me know, Sarah. This is helpful."

Sarah offered a faint smile before rising from her seat. "Sure thing! If you need me for anything, just let me know."

"Will do. Thanks again," Alex replied, watching as Sarah left the room, her words adding yet another layer to the mystery surrounding Henry Winters' death.

Alex leaned back in his chair, Sarah's conversation swirling through his mind. The pieces of the puzzle seemed to shift again, revealing new angles and raising fresh questions.

The caller's behavior is what really puzzled him. Why report the incident but withhold crucial details? Was it a genuine concern or a calculated move by a killer? The thought persisted—was the caller involved, perhaps feeling remorse or guilt that led to reporting the crime?

As he mulled over Sarah's account, an idea emerged. Could the caller have been the perpetrator, attempting to cover his tracks or divert attention? The abruptness of the call, the lack of cooperation—it all seemed too calculated.

Yet, his doubts were still there. What if the caller was genuinely trying to help, albeit rather reluctantly? The nuances of human behavior clouded the clarity Alex sought to find. The uncertainty gnawed at him, prompting more questions than answers.

His thoughts circled back to the motives behind the call. A sense of urgency to report yet an aversion to giving any crucial information—it was a paradox he couldn't easily reconcile.

The possibility that the killer was the caller was possibly a theory that demanded exploration. Alex made a mental note to dig deeper into the call records, hoping to uncover any additional leads that might shed light on the cryptic phone call.

Before leaving the station, Alex felt compelled to update Chief Brown on the developments in the case, even if they were just fragments. He made his way down the hallway, the soft rattle of the station accompanying his stride.

Upon reaching Chief Brown's office, Alex knocked lightly on the door. "Chief, it's Alex. May I come in?" he called out, waiting for permission before entering.

"Of course, come on in, Alex," Chief Brown replied, gesturing for him to take a seat.

Alex settled into the chair opposite Chief Brown, a sense of urgency underlining his words.

"Chief, I had a conversation with Sarah Jones. She revealed that the caller who reported Henry

Winters' situation in the park was rather elusive. A man, very straightforward but withholding crucial details."

Chief Brown listened attentively, his expression thoughtful. "That's an intriguing angle, Alex. The caller's behavior certainly raises suspicions. It's a thread we can't afford to ignore."

"Absolutely," Alex agreed, leaning forward slightly.

"I also spoke with Mrs. Winters earlier today. She seemed shocked by her husband's passing and mentioned that Henry had been deeply engrossed in the town's history. The journals, the cemetery visits—it all points to something significant."

Chief Brown nodded, contemplating the information. "There might be something in that history that someone didn't want Henry to uncover," he speculated.

"Exactly my thoughts," Alex affirmed, a flicker of determination in his eyes. "I'll be revisiting the case files and focusing on the history aspect. Hopefully, it will lead us somewhere."

"I hope it will," Chief responded. "While I have you here, I have noticed you and Detective Sinclair having a great connection. I also know you prefer to work alone. I just want you to know that we are a team here. Also, this is a tough case. If she is willing, I would take any help she can give."

Alex paused, thinking before responding, "She has really shown me what teamwork can be. Even though I have made this my case. I have enjoyed having her there. She is a great Detective with an eye for leads. If she offers any help, I'll be sure to take it."

With that, Alex rose from his seat, thanking the Chief with a nod of gratitude before leaving the office. The weight of the case rested heavily on his shoulders, driving him to uncover the truth behind Henry Winters' untimely demise.

As night began to fall, Alex made himself go to his car to go home. One thing he learned was that to have a sharp mind, you need to rest whenever possible.

As Alex eased into the driver's seat of his unmarked car, the familiar feel of the steering wheel grounded him as he closed the door. The quiet solitude within the vehicle provided a sanctuary for his thoughts.

As the engine of his car roared to life, Alex leaned back against the seat, letting his mind drift through the corridors of his memory. He recalled the journey that had brought him here—navigating the trials of police training, patrolling the streets, and finally earning his position as a detective.

His contemplation ventured into the lessons learned along the way. Some were hard-fought, etched into his experiences through trials and challenges. He remembered moments when missteps became lessons, learning the ropes of the profession through perseverance and determination.

Together with the recollections, a profound sense of gratitude enveloped him. The faces of mentors, colleagues, and friends flashed through his mind—the unwavering support and guidance they had offered. It was their collective influence that shaped him, instilling in him the values of camaraderie and solidarity.

With the weight of Henry Winters' case on his shoulders, Alex found comfort in the knowledge that he wasn't alone. The support system surrounding him, the capable colleagues, and the Chief's guidance—all stood as pillars of strength, reassuring him as he delved deeper into the enigma surrounding Henry's untimely death.

Alex's unmarked car rolled along the familiar streets of Pineworth, the town he had sworn to protect and serve. It was a town with a rich history, like an old blanket hand-woven with both great memories and terrifying secrets.

The town's evening canvas was now painted in shades of orange and lavender, the sun's final rays casting a beautiful glow upon the quiet streets. As Alex navigated through the roads, he observed the way of life that defined the town—the charming houses, each with its unique story, nestled side by side among tree-lined avenues.

He looked at the small storefronts decorated with twinkling lights, casting a warm feeling upon the locally owned shops. The amazing aroma of freshly brewed coffee from the local café wafted through the air, mixing well with the faint chatter of residents enjoying the evening.

Amongst the calming facade, he couldn't shake the questions of the day—the weight of the case, the unanswered questions, and the ceaseless pursuit of justice that had come to feel like his very existence.

The town's familiarity offered a strange proximity—the calm small town feel masking the underlying complexities that simmered beneath the surface. It was a place where life unfolded just like the shadows of the past, where every corner held tales of joy, sorrow, and unanswered mysteries.

As he neared his home, Alex's thoughts stayed on the dichotomy of the town—the seemingly soft exterior that hid the turbulent undercurrents lying just beneath. The familiar streets carried the weight of both nostalgia and the burden of the unknown, a constant reminder of the careful balance between serenity and unrest that defined the world that he lived in.

With a sigh, he parked his car in front of his residence, the town's mystic aura in his thoughts—a silent witness to the stories told by generations within its streets and the mysteries awaiting unraveling.

As Alex walked up the walkway of his home, a wave of silent nothing surrounded him. The evening cast an almost dark cloak over the neighborhood, but within the confines of his own space, thoughts drifted to deeper reflections.

Unlocking the front door, he stepped inside, greeted by the familiar comfort of his home. The solitude met him with a certain resonance, amplifying his thoughts. He found himself in a contemplative state, surrounded by the silent memories of the job's impact on his life.

It was in these moments of stillness that the weight of his profession bore down on him. The sacrifices made in the name of duty, the long hours devoted to solving cases, and the never-ending pursuit of justice all seemed to have left little room for personal pursuits.

The realization came heavily upon him. The relentless demands of the job had consumed much of his time and energy, leaving behind a figurative and literal void where personal aspirations and relationships might have thrived. His dedication to duty had often taken precedence, eclipsing the opportunity to engage in personal connections or even to start a family.

With a little bit of regret, Alex thought of the price he had paid—a sense of isolation that he seemed to be stuck in despite all the great activities of his career. He thought often of the roads not taken, the missed chances to nurture and grow personal relationships, and the sacrifice of a different kind of fulfillment.

The quietness of this evening seemed to multiply the silence within his own heart. He had learned to push those feelings deep down.

Alex settled onto the familiar embrace of his couch, seeking relaxation and a break from the day's complexities. He leaned back, attempting to find relief in the comfort of his living room, but again, he couldn't come to terms with his surroundings and failed to quell the ever-relentless churn of thoughts.

With each attempt to relax, the ins and outs of the case found their way back into his mind, refusing to grant him anyway to stop his brain. The memory of the crime scene, the clues, and the unanswered questions that remained haunting his consciousness like an unsolved puzzle waiting to be solved.

He closed his eyes one more time as if willing the details of the investigation to fade, but they persisted, each clue playing out vividly behind his eyelids. The journal, the history of the town, the evasive caller—it all merged into a web of intrigue, elusive and unexplainable.

The silence of his home itself even reverberated with the weight of the unsolved case, a constant reminder of the duty that demanded his attention, even within the confines of his sanctuary.

Frustration seeped into his thoughts, battling with his desire for relaxation. He yearned for that moment of ease, to silence the relentless barrage of the day's events that continued to haunt him. Maybe it was something he was missing in his own life that he yearned for.

Chapter 3
Clues Amidst Festivities

ALEX PARKED HIS CAR near the heart of Pineworth's bi-centennial event. The town square roared with activity—festive decorations on the streets, booths lined with historical artifacts, and an apparent air of celebration.

As he strolled along with the crowd, Alex immersed himself in the town's rich history displayed through exhibits and presentations. He then paused at a booth showcasing vintage photographs, each snapshot a small glimpse into the town's past. The faded images whispered stories of a bygone era, enticing Alex's curiosity.

Enamored in the displays, he found himself drawn to a certain lecture about the town's origins. The historian's words painted amazingly clear tales of settlers and founding families, narrating the town's evolution from a quiet settlement to the thriving community it had become.

Amidst the energetic festivities, Alex sought more than just commemoration. He sought answers, hoping that the town's history might hold clues important to the mysterious death of Henry Winters. There was a hunch he had that buried within the annals of the past lay keys to unlocking the secrets surrounding the enigmatic case.

As he perused the exhibits, he keenly observed the attendees, trying to figure out if anyone displayed a peculiar interest in specific aspects of the town's history. Every conversation, every artifact examined, held the potential to unravel the curiosity that is this case.

Alex approached the town hall, where an elderly gentleman with a warm smile stood by a display showcasing the town's history. The man, Mr. Beal, was a longtime resident and known for his wealth of knowledge about Pineworth's heritage. He even ran The Pineworth History Museum.

"Good afternoon, Detective Bennett," greeted Mr. Beal, extending a welcoming hand. "Are you here to dig into our town's intriguing past?"

"Yes sir, I am," replied Alex with a polite nod. "I have grown fascinated by the town's history. Could you share any tales about its founding or maybe any noteworthy events?"

With a sort of gleam in his eye, Mr. Beal began to recount the heroic origins of Pineworth. "Our town's genesis is a tale of resilience and courage. Legend has it that a group of settlers, who were seeking refuge from hardship, stumbled upon this land centuries ago."

Alex listened carefully, honestly captivated by the narrative.

"The settlers faced several challenges," continued Mr. Beal, "but they persevered. It was the valor of a few brave individuals that paved the way for our community to be what it is now."

As he spoke, Mr. Beal laid out a map of the town's founding, describing the many efforts of those early pioneers. "Their courage and determination against harsh adversity laid the foundation for what we cherish today."

"And that is one of the descendants over there," as he pointed towards a framed portrait of a distinguished figure, "he is Mayor Carter. He's a direct descendant of one of the founding families, carrying on their legacy."

Alex listened intently, trying to absorb every detail of the heroic saga that helped birth the town of Pineworth. The tale surprisingly resonated deeply, drawing parallels to the resilience he often encountered in his line of work—a testament to the enduring spirit that threaded through the town's history.

Alex thanked Mr. Beal for the excellent information, and his mind turned with thoughts as he mulled over the heroic founding story. As he walked away from the town hall, the narrative continued in his thoughts, almost forcing itself into his investigation.

He couldn't help but wonder about the significance of this historical tale. What lessons or connections from the town's courageous origins might provide insight into Henry Winters' sudden demise? It was an intriguing conundrum—a story steeped in bravery and resilience yet seemingly distant from the secrets surrounding the case.

Alex wandered through the town square, taking in all of the lively celebrations and festive atmosphere. The cheerful conversation of citizens of the town and the joyous ambiance of the bi-centennial events surrounded him, contrasting severely with the silent mystery he was tasked to solve.

The narrative of the founding's bravery continued to come back in his mind, a reminder of the enduring spirit that the community stood for. While the historical account seemed distant from the current investigation, Alex couldn't shake the feeling that hidden within those valorous tales might lie subtle clues or wisdom relevant to his quest for answers.

With a few thoughtful expressions, he made mental notes, thinking about the potential relevance the founding story had in the broader context of the case. The puzzle pieces of history and contemporary events danced tantalizingly at the edge of his consciousness, asking for connections to be made.

The intrigued detective wandered through the busy bi-centennial event, catching sight of Nathan Reynolds engaged in conversation with Sarah Jones and her daughter, Lizzy. Nathan, noticing Alex, waved him over.

"Hey, Alex! Lizzy, this is Detective Bennett, a detective who works with me and your mom." Nathan said, introducing Alex to Lizzy.

"Hi there, Lizzy," Alex greeted warmly, offering a friendly smile.

"Nice to meet you, Detective," Lizzy replied, returning the smile.

Nathan turned back to Alex. "How's it going? Anything new in town?"

"Just taking in the festivities for now, Nathan," Alex replied. "Haven't stumbled onto any mysteries yet."

Sarah nodded, chiming in, "Well, if anyone can solve a mystery, it's you."

They engaged in light conversation, discussing the lively atmosphere of the event and sharing a few anecdotes about the historical exhibits on display. Amidst the joyful ambiance, Alex found a momentary break from the weight of his usual caseload.

After a pleasant conversation, Alex bid them farewell with a casual wave. "Enjoy the festivities, folks. Have a great day!"

Continuing through the crowded event, he stumbled upon an exhibit dedicated to the founding families of Pineworth. Displayed prominently were the Winters, Carters, Phillips, and Thompsons—the pillars upon which the town's rich history was built. Each family's story, etched with tales of perseverance and contribution, held a significant place in Pineworth's legacy.

Alex studied the photographs and artifacts, intrigued by the intricate details of the town's past. The pride of the families resonated in the displays, a testament to their enduring commitment to the community. Amidst the celebration, these historical portraits served as a reminder of the town's roots and the values it held dear.

As he observed, the ties between the founding families and the present-day residents seemed embedded into the DNA of the town, connecting the past to the present in a way that carried on through generations.

"Is there something about these families that Henry found out?" he wondered.

As Alex continued his leisurely stroll through the town square, he was approached by a well-dressed man with an agreeable demeanor. "Excuse me, Detective Bennett," the man greeted with a wide smile, extending his hand.

"Michael, how are you today?" replied Alex, reciprocating the handshake.

"I'm great, enjoying the show. My brother made sure this was a great day for everyone."

Michael Carter, the mayor's younger brother, exuded an air of confidence. His demeanor was warm, and his friendly manner put Alex at ease. It was evident that Michael enjoyed being an integral part of the town, much like his esteemed sibling.

"Hope you're enjoying our bi-centennial celebration," remarked Michael, gesturing toward the festive activities around them.

"It's quite the event," agreed Alex, taking in the lively atmosphere. "It's an honor to be part of this occasion."

As they exchanged pleasantries, Michael shared some stories of his own about the town's history and the significance of the bi-centennial celebration. His likable nature and deep-rooted pride in Pineworth's heritage shone through as he spoke, adding depth to the importance of the event.

As they continued their conversation, Michael's eyes shined with a sense of pride as he spoke about the Carter family's role in Pineworth's history. "You know, Detective Bennett," Michael began, his tone carrying a hint of nostalgia, "our family played a pivotal role in establishing this town. The Carters were among the first settlers here, striving to create a community that thrived on unity and progress."

Alex nodded, intrigued by Michael's recounting of the town's founding. "It's fascinating to hear about the town's origins. The dedication of families like yours laid the foundation for what Pineworth is today."

Michael nodded in agreement. "You bet our forefathers believed in hard work, resilience, and a strong sense of community. They strived to create a place where everyone could prosper and hopefully find a sense of belonging."

As Michael spoke of the Carter family's role in Pineworth's history, Alex's curiosity began to show. "Michael, I've come across some references to the other founding families—like the Winters, Phillips, and Thompsons—in various town records. They, too, seem to lay a pretty steep claim to the town's inception."

A subtle shift in Michael's demeanor was noticeable. His expression turned from a smile to something that looked like he was getting more serious, hinting at a deeper sentiment. "Ah, yes, the Winters, Phillips, and Thompsons. They have their versions, as all families do. But the truth is Detective, they often try to claim their prominence by overshadowing the contributions made by the Carters."

There was a sense of conviction in Michael's voice as he continued, "It's a common occurrence, you see. Each family boasts about being the 'first,' vying for recognition in the town's history books. But sometimes, they forget the sacrifices and efforts of others."

"Thank you for sharing your insights, Michael," Alex said, bidding farewell to the mayor's brother. As he walked away, he couldn't shake off the subtle shift in Michael's demeanor or the revelation about the town's historical families.

Michael's mention of the inter-family rivalries and attempts to claim prominence in the town's history stirred a thought in Alex's mind. Could the friction between these families somehow be linked to Henry's tragic demise?

Keeping a mental note of this newfound knowledge, Alex reflected on the possible implications. He contemplated delving deeper into the connections between Pineworth's prominent families and the circumstances surrounding Henry's death. It felt like a pivotal clue, urging him to explore the town's history further in his investigation.

With this new perspective, Alex continued his stroll through the teeming bi-centennial celebration, his mind now navigating the intricacies of the town's past in search of answers to the present mystery.

During the lively festivities, Alex spotted Matthew Winters, Henry's son, standing by a historical exhibit. Approaching him discreetly, Alex engaged in conversation, hoping to gather more insights.

"Hi, Matthew," greeted Alex, offering a warm smile. "I hope you're enjoying the celebration."

Matthew reciprocated the greeting, though his demeanor hinted at the weight of recent events. "Trying to, Detective Bennett," Matthew replied, his voice tinged with a mix of sorrow and determination.

"I wanted to ask you something, Matthew," Alex began gently. "Did your father ever mention any disputes or issues with the other founding families?"

Matthew paused for a moment, reflecting on his father's words. "Dad was always trying to prove something, you know? He'd often tell me that while the Winters might not have been the wealthiest, we were always the kindest and the hardest working."

There was a sense of pride in Matthew's tone as he spoke about his family's values. Alex noted the sentiment behind Henry's words and considered how deeply entrenched the family pride was in Pineworth's history.

Listening attentively, Alex nodded as Matthew shared more about his father's discoveries. "He found an old journal in my grandfather's belongings, something about the town's history," Matthew explained. "Dad was thrilled when he stumbled upon it. He practically immersed himself in it."

"He studied it all the time, trying to decipher its contents," Matthew continued, recalling his father's deep interest. "He believed it held valuable information about our family's role in the town's founding. It was as if he was on a mission to uncover some hidden truth."

Alex noted the significance of the journal in Henry's life. It seemed that Henry's fervent study of the historical document might have held clues to the family's ties to the town's origins. This new detail added depth to the investigation, sparking an interest in the contents of the journal.

"Thank you for answering my questions, Matthew," Alex says.

"I know this has been hard on you." he continued.

"It has, but I know he is somewhere looking down, enjoying this celebration. He loved this town." Matthew responded.

After saying goodbye, Alex took in the rest of the event. He couldn't help but feel as though this was the type of gathering the killer would be.

Alex knew where his investigation was going to head next. The journal might give him more information on the motive for the crime.

Chapter 4
The Journal

The morning after the bi-centennial celebration, Alex sat in his office, the small red journal that had been found with Henry at the scene laid out before him. The worn leather cover bore the name "Thomas Winters" inscribed in faded gold lettering, revealing it as a cherished possession of Henry's grandfather.

Flipping through the yellowed pages, Alex scanned the handwritten entries. The journal chronicled the life and times of Thomas Winters, providing a vivid account of the town's inception. Each entry painted a picture of Pineworth's early days, detailing the struggles and triumphs of the founding families—the Winters, Carters, Phillips, and Thompsons.

Thomas's meticulous writings referenced the interactions and conflicts between the influential families, each vying for prominence in the town's history. His words shed light on the town's humble beginnings, sharing tales of unity, prosperity, and the pursuit of distinction among the founding members.

Amidst the historical recount, Alex stumbled upon intriguing passages that hinted at hidden tensions and unsolved disputes between the families. References to a certain incident alluded to in veiled language hinted at a rift that threatened to tear apart the unity the town was founded upon.

Fascinated by the intricate details within the journal, Alex recognized its value as a key to unlocking the secrets buried deep within the town's past. He meticulously poured over each entry, absorbing the essence of Thomas Winters' chronicles and the legacy they held.

Following the poignant entry that read, "We had to do what we had to do for the sake of the town," Alex turned the fragile pages, feeling a growing sense of anticipation. As he reached the spot where the torn-out page was supposed to be, he was met with a palpable absence—an eerie void amidst the otherwise meticulously recorded history.

The torn-out page stood as a stark reminder of a deliberate attempt to conceal something crucial. Its absence posed a perplexing puzzle, leaving an unsettling feeling that a vital piece of information had been purposefully erased.

Alex pondered over the enigmatic words preceding the missing page, trying to decipher their significance. The cryptic message, shrouded in the vagueness of the journal's entries, hinted at a decision made, a sacrifice or compromise undertaken in the name of the town.

With the torn-out page in mind, Alex realized that the answer to Henry's tragic end might be nestled within those lost words. The missing piece was an integral part of the puzzle, holding the key to unraveling the mystery that plagued Pineworth.

After going through the journal, Alex realized he needed to speak with someone from each family mentioned as a founding family.

He began his quest by visiting Ethan Phillips, the venerable figure among the Phillips family and a judge in the Pineworth.

Arriving at the stately home of the Phillips, Alex was greeted by an aura of tradition and legacy that emanated from the grand estate. The abode, a testament to the family's deep roots in Pineworth, exuded a sense of heritage and authority.

As he approached the imposing front door, Alex mentally prepared himself for the conversation that lay ahead. He rang the doorbell, awaiting Judge Phillips' arrival with a mix of anticipation and curiosity, eager to glean insights into the town's past from one of its most influential figures.

As Phillips welcomed Alex into his residence, the distinguished aura of the place reflected the Phillips family's significant standing in Pineworth's history. They settled in the study, surrounded by the mementos of the town's past, with aged photographs and artifacts adorning the walls.

With a thoughtful expression, Alex broached the topic of the town's history and the recent events concerning Henry Winters. Ethan leaned forward, his demeanor changing as he recalled Henry's mention of the journal during one of the annual gatherings.

"Ah, yes," Ethan began, his voice tinged with reminiscence. "Henry did bring up the journal during our last gathering about four months ago. Mentioned something about uncovering some truths from our ancestors' accounts."

Ethan paused for a moment, the memories of that night resurfacing. "It caused quite a stir, I must say," he continued. "Buddy Thompson, he was quite upset, though I never heard firsthand what was in that journal. He stormed out after some heated words were exchanged."

Alex took note of Ethan's account, the mention of Buddy Thompson's reaction piquing his interest. The connection between the journal and the Thompson family's reaction seemed significant, hinting at a possible link to the tension surrounding Henry's findings.

Intrigued by Ethan's revelation, Alex leaned in, his interest piqued by the conflict that had arisen at the gathering. "Do you recall what particularly upset Buddy Thompson about Henry's mention of the journal?" Alex inquired, his gaze fixed on Ethan, hoping for a glimpse into the root of the discord.

Ethan looked around in contemplation. "It's hard to say exactly," he began, searching his memory for details. "Buddy's always been quite protective of his family's legacy. Anything that might challenge or tarnish their reputation seemed to strike a nerve with him."

"There's a deep-rooted pride among the founding families," Ethan continued, his tone reflective. "I reckon any revelations that could cast a shadow on their history would ruffle some feathers."

Alex absorbed Ethan's words, recognizing the inherent sensitivity surrounding the town's heritage. The protective stance of the founding families only deepened the mystery surrounding Henry's findings and the torn-out page from the journal. The puzzle seemed to grow more intricate with each piece of information uncovered.

Before leaving, Alex thanked Ethan for his insights, knowing that Buddy Thompson's reaction could hold vital clues to untangling the truth behind Henry's untimely demise.

Alex knew that his next interview was obvious. Buddy Thompson.

As Alex arrived at Buddy Thompson's residence, the notable businessman and proprietor of several town stores greeted him with a cordial yet guarded demeanor. Alex wasted no time in broaching the sensitive topic, asking about the confrontation between Buddy and Henry.

"Buddy, I'm investigating Henry Winters' death, and I need your insight," Alex began, his tone earnest. "What happened between you and Henry a few months ago?"

Buddy's expression darkened memories of the heated exchange resurfacing. "Henry started making wild claims," Buddy retorted, his voice tinged with frustration. "He accused our families of fabricating the town's history and said it was all a lie."

"He was obsessed with that blasted journal of his," Buddy continued, a hint of exasperation in his voice. "Trying to dig up old stories and discredit the founding families. It was disrespectful, a disgrace to our heritage."

Alex took note of Buddy's vehement reaction, the vehement defense of his family's legacy hinting at the depth of emotion behind Henry's accusations. The fervent denial and defensiveness among the founding families added another layer to the mystery surrounding the torn-out page and the journal.

"I would rather not go into it." he continued.

"I understand." Alex replied.

Alex probed further, his tone measured. "Buddy, did Henry's claims about the town's history anger you or anyone else enough to harm him?"

Buddy's response was swift and resolute. "No, no one from our families would ever resort to such drastic measures," he affirmed, shaking his head. "Sure, Henry had a way of ruffling feathers with his talk, but no one would go to such extremes."

"Henry always had a knack for stirring the pot, questioning everything," Buddy continued a tinge of annoyance in his voice. "But that's as far as it went. No one would hurt him over it."

Alex nodded, taking in Buddy's emphatic denial.

The words mirrored Ethan Phillips' earlier assurance, affirming that while Henry's accusations might have provoked discomfort, they didn't drive anyone to resort to violence.

After bidding farewell to Mr. Thompson, Alex decided to pay a visit to Mayor Seth Carter. He was hoping that the Mayor was present when the heated exchange occurred.

Alex drove through the quiet streets of Pineworth, making his way to City Hall, where Mayor Seth Carter conducted his duties. The Carter family, one of the prominent names in town, held a long-standing history within the community.

As he entered the grandeur of City Hall, Alex was ushered into the mayor's office. Mayor Seth Carter welcomed him warmly, recognizing Alex's reputation as a diligent investigator.

"Seth, I need your help with something," Alex began, getting straight to the point. "I'm looking into Henry Winters' death, and I've been gathering information about an incident a few months ago involving him and the founding families. Do you recall that?"

Mayor Carter, a venerable figure in town, leaned forward, his brow furrowed in thought. "Ah, yes, I remember," he replied, contemplating the recollection. "Henry was quite insistent about

his findings. He claimed he had evidence that challenged the established history of our town."

"Can you shed some light on what he discovered?" Alex inquired, hopeful that the mayor might provide a critical piece to the puzzle.

"I'm afraid I can't be of much help there," Mayor Carter admitted, his expression solemn. "He never divulged the specifics to me, but it was clear he believed it was a significant revelation."

As the conversation unfolded, Alex realized that Henry's findings were central to the case, yet the details remained elusive. He thanked Mayor Carter for his time, appreciating the insight gleaned about the intensity of Henry's beliefs.

As the discussion progressed, Alex turned his attention to another potential lead. "Seth, I noticed Michael Carter seemed upset when I spoke with him at the town festival. Any idea why he would harbor such feelings towards Henry?"

Mayor Carter sighed, his shoulders slumping ever so slightly. "The Carters and Winters have a history of disagreements, as do many of the founding families. It's not uncommon for tensions to arise, especially when discussions about the town's history take place."

He continued, "Michael and Henry had their differences. That's no secret. Disagreements over the past, family legacies, and the importance of our town's history. But hurting Henry? No, I can't see Michael doing that. Dislike, yes. Violence, no."

Alex took note of Mayor Carter's words, recognizing the intricate web of conflicts woven through the fabric of Pineworth's history. The interplay of family legacies and differing perspectives added layers of complexity to the investigation.

"I appreciate your candor, Seth. If you remember anything else or hear of any developments, please let me know," Alex requested, rising from his chair.

Mayor Carter nodded in assurance, understanding the weight of the situation. "Of course, Alex. I want to see justice served for Henry as much as anyone else in this town."

As Alex left City Hall, he couldn't shake the feeling that beneath the surface of Pineworth's picturesque exterior lay a pool of hidden tensions and long-buried secrets, all waiting to be unraveled.

As Alex bid farewell to Mayor Seth Carter, he couldn't help but inject a touch of humor into the conversation. "By the way, Seth, I must say, the re-election signs scattered around the town square are quite the spectacle. It's almost like a mini forest of political aspirations out there."

Mayor Carter chuckled, appreciating the lighthearted remark. "Ah, yes, the joys of small-town politics. Keeps things interesting, doesn't it? Feel free to grab one on your way out – they make excellent souvenirs!"

With a shared laugh, Alex exited City Hall, leaving the swarming atmosphere of the political hub behind. As he strolled through the town square, the colorful array of election signs caught his eye. Each sign, a testament to the democratic heartbeat of Pineworth, seemed to beckon voters to join in the spirited dance of local governance.

Alex couldn't help but muse on the peculiar charm of his town, a place where political campaigns took on a quaint and familiar air. The signs, like sentinels of civic engagement, stood proudly, each vying for attention in the prelude to the upcoming election.

As he walked away, Alex pondered the intricate dance between politics and the darker mysteries that lurked in the shadows. The juxtaposition of electoral enthusiasm against the backdrop of a murder investigation underscored the multifaceted nature of life in Pineworth.

After leaving the Mayor's office, Alex decided to clear his head and drive around town. He always found stopping to take in the small-town scenery helped him focus.

As Alex cruised through the familiar streets of Pineworth, his mind came back to the stark contrast between the fancy estates of the founding families and the more modest residences scattered throughout the town. The architectural disparity mirrored the socioeconomic divisions that had persisted for generations.

The sprawling mansions, adorned with manicured lawns and imposing gates, stood as symbols of the entrenched power held by families like the Winters, Carters, Phillips, and Thompsons. Meanwhile, nestled in the shadows of these grand structures, the homes of the town's working-class residents bore witness to a different reality.

Rows of neatly kept but smaller houses lined the streets, telling stories of perseverance, hard work, and community bonds. The dichotomy between privilege and struggle was unmistakable, casting a mist over the town's social landscape.

As Alex observed the disparities, he couldn't help but reflect on how these economic divisions might play into the broader narrative of Pineworth. The founding families, with their interwoven histories and conflicts, seemed to hold the threads of influence tightly in their grasp.

The detective pondered whether this socioeconomic imbalance had fueled the tensions within the town, contributing to the animosity and disagreements that had been hinted at during his interviews. Pineworth, it appeared, carried its own set of burdens, hidden behind the facades of picturesque landscapes and historic charm.

The police station was unusually quiet as Alex arrived. Making his way to his office, he spotted Chief Brown engrossed in paperwork at his desk. The seasoned chief looked up, acknowledging Alex's presence with a nod.

"Alex," Chief Brown greeted, his voice a steady baritone. "What did you uncover today? Any leads on Henry's case?"

Taking a seat across from the chief, Alex began to share his findings from the conversations with Ethan Phillips, Buddy Thompson, and Mayor Seth Carter. He delved into the peculiar dynamics between the founding families, the potential motives, and the palpable tension that seemed to underpin the town's social fabric.

Chief Brown listened intently, his expression thoughtful as he absorbed the nuances of Alex's discoveries. After a moment of silence, he leaned back in his chair, folding his hands together.

"This town has a long history, Alex. The power dynamics between those families have shaped Pineworth in more ways than one. But motive alone doesn't solve a case. We need concrete evidence. Keep digging, and let's see if we can connect the dots."

"So you really think it is possible? I mean, these guys have a great life here. Why would they want to mess that up?" Alex questions out loud.

"It's a possibility," the chief conceded, "but don't let possibilities blind you to probabilities. Not everything is as it appears, and sometimes the answers are in the last place you'd expect."

"Thank you, Chief," Alex states, sensing the end of the conversation.

Alex rose from his seat, a nod of gratitude exchanged with Chief Brown. As he left the chief's office, he could not help but feel a certain awkwardness of the quiet that surrounded him.

As the day came to an end, Alex felt a feeling of being on the right path. He was ready to close the case. Whatever the cost.

Chapter 5
Retracing the Beat

The sun had barely painted the morning sky like strokes of pink and gold paint when Alex woke to the gentle melody of his alarm. The rhythmic beep, once a call to duty, now marked the beginning of his day as a detective. The transition from the rigid routine of a police officer to the nuances of a detective's life was still settling within him.

As he pulled on a crisp shirt and tie, Alex couldn't help but reflect on the simplicity of his morning routine compared to the unpredictability awaiting him at the precinct. Gone were the days of donning the familiar uniform, a symbol of authority and service. Instead, his attire now mirrored the civilians he served—a subtle reminder of the new chapter in his career.

Alex has been a detective for the department for five years now.

It seems like yesterday he was on the beat in the city taking calls. He loved the nearly four years on the beat. It showed him a lot about the town and policing in general.

Alex filled his coffee mug up to the brim. The feel of the cup turning warm brings an equally warm feeling to him. As he takes the first sip, he closes his eyes.

As he drank, he reflected on the case that had led him to become a detective at such a young age. Many have to wait longer than four years to be given such an opportunity.

He let his mind take him back to that fateful call nearly five years ago.

The patrol cruised along as Alex, unit 8-Delta, navigated the quiet streets of Pineworth. Dispatch's voice breaks through the monotony, a call to action at the intersection of West Main Street and the unknown.

"Unit 8-Delta, we've got a situation at 782 West Main Street, MapleFuel. The caller reports a possible disturbance. Proceed with caution."

The name 'MapleFuel' rings out in the crisp night air, a beacon guiding Alex toward a narrative unfolding at the gas station. The flickering lights of the establishment come into view, casting an amber glow on the asphalt. The rhythmic thumping of the patrol car's tires becomes a prelude to the unknown challenges awaiting him.

Pulling into the MapleFuel station, Alex scanned the surroundings—the pumps standing like sentinels, the convenience store's rusty windows revealing nothing but shadows within. Dispatch relays additional details, the storyline evolving with each passing moment. The night, once serene, now pulses with the potential for unpredictability.

As Alex approaches the unappealing gas station, the dim glow of the convenience store lights reveals an unsettling scene. A young boy, no older than an elementary school student, lies motionless on the cold asphalt. The night, once filled with the loud warble of the patrol car and the distant wail of the town, now reflects an eerie silence.

Adrenaline courses through Alex's veins as he surveys the area. His training is kicking in. The scene must be secured, evidence preserved, and the truth unraveled from the darkness that shrouds it. The boy's lifeless form prompts a surge of determination in Alex—a promise to bring justice to a life cut short.

Gently but methodically, he sets up a perimeter, ensuring no one disturbs the scene's integrity. The flickering fluorescent lights above cast a solemn glow on the surroundings, turning the ordinary gas station into a somber stage for a tragic tale.

Alex's hands move with purpose as he dons latex gloves, bending down to examine the young victim. The harsh reality of a gunshot wound is stark in the dim light, a harsh reminder of the unforgiving nature of his job. His radio crackles with updates from dispatch, each piece of information adding depth to the unfolding narrative.

As Alex meticulously goes through his on-scene investigation, memories of his encounters with a local gang flash vividly. It wasn't too long ago that the same streets witnessed a different kind of darkness – the menacing presence of those who chose violence as their language.

The gas station scene, now marked by the tragedy of a young life extinguished, draws an unsettling parallel to the encounters Alex had with a local gang. He recalls the pattern they followed – a brutal act followed by hasty disposal of the weapon, tossed callously into a nearby ditch.

Amidst the rows of the streetlights, Alex's keen eyes spot a glint of metal in the ditch nearby. Instinctively, he narrows his focus on the discovery, his heart beating faster. The moment's weight hangs in the air as he carefully reaches down and retrieves the discarded weapon.

The cold steel of the gun, now in his gloved hands, sends a shiver down his spine. It's a chilling artifact, a tangible piece of the violence that has stained the quiet streets of Pineworth. The memories of his previous encounters with a similar brand of cruelty flicker in his mind like haunting shadows, connecting the dots between the past and the present.

Examining the firearm with a practiced eye, Alex notes its make and model. Every detail becomes a crucial piece in the puzzle he's determined to solve. He can almost feel the weight of the responsibility on his shoulders – the duty to bring justice to the young victim and closure to a community shaken by tragedy.

The gun, once a tool of destruction, now becomes a key piece of evidence in the pursuit of truth.

Alex carefully places it in an evidence bag, sealing the fate of the weapon that may hold the answers to the current crime and the relation to his past.

As he secures the evidence, the night's silence is broken only by the howling of a city wrestling with its demons and the solemn promise of justice being served.

Back in the present, the memories of that pivotal case resurface in Alex's mind, like fragments of a puzzle falling into place. The murder of Marcus was a turning point, not just for the community but also for Alex himself. As he navigated the twists and turns of the investigation, Chief Brown recognized something in him – a tenacity, an innate ability to seek the truth.

The traces of that fateful night were recurrent, and it wasn't long before Chief Brown, impressed by Alex's investigative skills, encouraged him to take the next step in his career. The detective position became a beacon, a chance for Alex to delve deeper into the complexities of crime and justice.

The transition from patrolling the streets to investigating their darker secrets significantly shifted Alex's professional journey. It was a choice that reflected his dedication to upholding the law and his commitment to unraveling the mysteries that cast shadows over Pineworth.

Now, as he reflects on that pivotal moment, Alex contemplates the evolution of his career – from the uniformed officer responding to calls to the detective entrusted with solving the murder of Henry Winters.

The main thing he missed about being on the beat was the many different people he would encounter. He loved helping the people of the community. Unlike now, where most of his day was consumed thinking about a single case, back then, it was unknown. The calls would come in—all types of situations.

The decision to become a detective was never one he thought would come so soon. He is thankful every day for his career. Some people go a lifetime not finding their true calling. Due to a bit of encouragement and hard work, he could see his.

Alex arrived at the station like any other day. He was going over the evidence of the Sinters case once again. While doing so, his mind thought back again to the day he decided to become an officer.

Growing up, he was never the little kid who always wanted to be a cop. Quite the opposite. He was a problem child in school.

After barely escaping high school, Alex remembers his father approaching him and saying, "Why don't you join the police force?"

Alex thought he was insane and replied, "Why would I do that? I am not the type".

Then, his father told him something that he would remember forever. "Son, in this world, we only have one shot to make a difference. You can live your life not caring and being a part of the issue, or you can be a part of the solution that helps this world be better."

Was it that his father saw something in him that he couldn't see in himself?

Maybe so. Either way, it led him to the case that lay before him on his desk now. All he wants to do now is solve this mystery and help bring justice to the Winters family.

While sitting there, Alex came to the realization that the only way to proceed was to delve deeper into the town's past. Possibly even find out the darker past of the founding families.

Chapter 6
Shadows of Yesteryears

AS ALEX ARRIVED AT the museum, the weathered exterior seemed to sag under the weight of forgotten tales. Mr. Beal, the town historian, awaited him in the dimly lit foyer. Together, they ventured into the archives, where the scent of aging paper hung in the air.

The room was a treasure trove of the town's history—stacks of dusty volumes, yellowed documents, and the soft rustle of forgotten stories. Mr. Beal, a custodian of Pineworth's past, guided Alex through the labyrinth of historical records.

While cracking open the fragile pages of dusty ledgers, the detective was transported back in time. Faded ink on brittle paper told tales of Pineworth's founding families, their aspirations, and the intricacies that shaped the town's destiny. Sunlight filtered through time-stained windows, casting a soft glow on the mysteries concealed within the archives.

Amidst the fading parchment and the hushed whispers of history, Alex's discerning eyes fell upon an old, weathered document—an agreement that brought back the long-standing connection between the Carter and Winter families. Intrigued, he carefully unfolded the brittle pages and gestured for Mr. Beal to join him.

As the detective and the custodian of history examined the fragile document, the ink seemed to come alive with the tales of a bygone era. Mr. Beal, with a hint of nostalgia in his voice, began to unravel the story embedded within the faded text.

"This land agreement, Detective," Mr. Beal explained, "dates back to the very foundations of Pineworth. It delineates the boundaries and shared responsibilities between the Carter and Winter families, two pillars upon which our town was built."

Alex listened intently as the historian detailed the terms of the agreement—a testament to the collaborative spirit that once flourished between the founding families. The document spoke of a time when the Carters and Winters, bound by more than mere proximity, worked hand in hand for the prosperity of Pineworth.

As they perused the text, Alex's investigative instincts tingled. Could this document hold the key to the mysteries surrounding Henry's demise? Were there hidden nuances that eluded casual observation? The detective posed these questions to Mr. Beal, hoping to extract insights from the custodian's wealth of knowledge.

With each revelation, the agreement painted a portrait of a harmonious past that seemed at odds with the recent discord between the families. Alex sensed that beneath the ink-stained surface lay a narrative that had evolved over time—a narrative entangled with secrets, shifting loyalties, and unforeseen fractures.

As Alex delved deeper into the details of the land agreement, a sudden revelation unfolded—the delicate balance of the past seemed to teeter under the weight of obscured truths. He raised an eyebrow, focusing intently on Mr. Beal's revelation about the Carters potentially overstepping the bounds set forth in the agreement.

"Wait a minute," Mr. Beal muttered, his eyes narrowing at the intricacies of the aged document. "It appears that the Carters might have taken more land than the agreement stipulates."

Alex's detective instincts kicked in as he scrutinized the details. The potential discrepancy hinted at the erosion of the once-pristine harmony between the founding families. The subtle power dynamics woven into the town's history were now exposed, challenging the idyllic narrative of unity.

"What does this mean for the town today?" Alex inquired, contemplating the implications of the apparent deviation from the original agreement.

Mr. Beal sighed, recognizing the significance of this newfound revelation. "It's not uncommon for disputes to arise over land matters. Over time, these issues can fester and breed resentment. The agreement was a pact to ensure mutual cooperation, but as with any document, interpretations can vary."

As the detective absorbed this information, he considered the possibility that the ancient land agreement might be a key element in understanding the recent turbulence between the Carter and Winter families. The town's roots, seemingly solidified in unity, now hinted at a clandestine web of rivalry that could hold the key to Henry's tragic fate.

"Mr. Beal," Alex began, steering the conversation toward the mysterious journal, "I came across a journal, Thomas Winters's, to be exact. There's a missing page right after a cryptic entry that reads, 'We had to do what we had to do for the sake of the town.' Any idea what might be on that torn-out page?"

Mr. Beal's eyes widened slightly at the mention of the journal. "The missing page, you say?" he mused, rubbing his chin. "Well, in my years of sifting through town records, I've heard whispers about disagreements between the founding families. There might be something crucial on that page—perhaps an agreement or a decision that was deemed too controversial to be left in the open."

Alex's curiosity deepened as he pressed further, "Do you think this land agreement could be related to what's on that torn-out page? It seems like there might be a connection."

Mr. Beal squinted at the pages that were still there, carefully examining the faded ink. "It's challenging to say definitively," he admitted, adjusting his glasses. "Land agreements were common back then, and many disputes arose over property boundaries. This specific agreement seems straightforward, but whether it holds the key to the torn-out page's mystery... Well, that's a puzzle we'll have to solve."

The detective nodded, absorbing the information. The town's intricate history appeared to be a fraud with hidden conflicts and long-buried secrets. If there was a chance that the torn-out page held crucial details about a past decision, Alex knew he needed to follow this thread, even if it meant navigating through the complex dynamics of the founding families.

"Mr. Beal," Alex inquired, "do you have any records or information about what existed here before the town was founded? Anything that predates the establishment of Pineworth?"

The historian had a look of doubt on his face. "I'm afraid most of our records focus on the town's founding and the subsequent history. It's challenging to find detailed information on what might have been here before. Perhaps there are some local legends or oral histories that have been passed down, but as for official records, they are quite limited."

Alex nodded, understanding the constraints of historical documentation. The detective realized that he might have to dig deeper, exploring alternative sources and seeking out individuals who might hold pieces of the puzzle in their memories or family stories.

"MR. BEAL, AMONG ALL the founding families, who is the most senior member I could talk to? Someone who might have a broader understanding of the town's history, especially its early days," Alex inquired.

Beal pondered for a moment before responding, "Well, if we're considering the eldest among the founding families, that would be Daniel Carter. He's been a prominent figure in the community for many years. I believe he could provide valuable insights into the history of Pineworth."

Armed with this information, Alex decided to pay a visit to Daniel Carter, hoping that the elder statesman might hold the key to unlocking the mysteries hidden within the town's past.

The tires of Alex's unmarked car crunched on the gravel driveway as he pulled up to Daniel Carter's ranch. A sprawling landscape unfolded before him, reflecting the grandeur of Pineworth's history. A gentle breeze rustled the leaves of nearby trees, and the distant lowing of cattle provided a tranquil backdrop to the meeting that awaited him.

Approaching the front door, Alex took a moment to gather his thoughts. He knocked, and after a brief pause, the door swung open, revealing a weathered yet welcoming face.

"Mr. Carter, my name is Detective Alex Bennett. I'm here to talk to you about the history of Pineworth and some recent events that might be connected to it," Alex explained as he extended his hand in greeting.

Daniel Carter, a patriarch whose life seemed interwoven with the very fabric of the town, offered a firm handshake. "Come on in, Detective. I've lived in this town for the better part of my life; there's not much I don't know. What can I help you with?" he inquired, leading Alex into a cozy living room adorned with family photographs and memorabilia.

Seated in the comfortable living room, surrounded by the ghosts of generations past, Alex steered the conversation toward the delicate topic of Pineworth's social dynamics.

"Mr. Carter, in my investigation, I've come across certain historical elements that seem to suggest some tensions among the founding families. Have there been any long-standing feuds or disagreements that you're aware of?" Alex inquired, maintaining a respectful tone.

Daniel Carter's gaze shifted momentarily as if contemplating the weight of history.

"Well, Detective, you're talking about a town that's seen its fair share of disagreements since 1824. Families, even the founding ones, don't always see eye to eye. But, as far as I know, we've always managed to keep our disputes civil. There might be disagreements, but blood is thicker than water, as they say."

Alex nodded thoughtfully, recognizing the delicate balance between truth and the town's unwritten code of loyalty. "I appreciate your honesty, Mr. Carter. It's just that I've been trying to piece together some recent events that might have roots in the past. Specifically, I'm looking into an incident involving Thomas Winters' journal and a torn-out page."

The mention of the torn page brought a flicker of recognition to Daniel Carter's eyes. "Thomas Winters' journal, you say? That old thing has been a topic of discussion lately. What exactly are you trying to find out?"

"Do you know what was in the journal?" Alex asks.

"Look, Henry thought he had something that could change things. The reality is that it was a fantasy." Mr. Carter replied.

Mr. Carter's response seemed measured as if he trod carefully through the layers of history. Alex absorbed the information, considering the possibility that the torn page might hold more significance than initially thought.

"I understand, Mr. Carter. I'm trying to piece together the puzzle, and every bit of information helps. If there's anything you recall, even if it seems insignificant, it could aid in resolving this case," Alex said, maintaining his focus on the task at hand.

Daniel sighed, a trace of weariness etched on his face. "Detective, Pineworth is a town with its roots firmly embedded in the past. Sometimes, those roots run deep, and unearthing them can stir up more than anticipated. As for the journal, I can't say I remember much. Thomas Winters had his views, but nothing that should have led to harm."

As the conversation unfolded, Alex sensed the weight of the town's history bearing down on the present investigation. He thanked Daniel for his cooperation and assured him that he would explore all leads to uncover the truth.

Leaving the Carter ranch, Alex couldn't shake the feeling that the answers he sought were entwined with the secrets woven into Pineworth's foundation.

The torn-out page, the accusations in Thomas Winters' journal, and the intricacies of the founding families hinted at foul play.

After leaving the ranch, Alex decided to revisit the crime scene.

The scene was quiet, the remnants of yesterday's festival now replaced by the sober reality of an ongoing investigation. Alex walked through the park, the same path he had taken the day before, retracing his steps. He examined the area where Henry Winters was found, visualizing the sequence of events that led to the tragedy.

Despite the picturesque surroundings, the park now bore the weight of a dark secret. The beauty of the bi-centennial event contrasted sharply with the unresolved questions surrounding the town's past and Henry's discovery.

Alex meticulously surveyed the grounds, looking for any overlooked details or clues that might shed light on the motive behind the murder.

Alex retraced his steps, recalling the details shared by the witness about the man she saw standing near the crime scene. He followed her description, navigating through the park to the spot where she had pointed.

As he approached the designated area, he observed the surroundings with a fresh perspective. The trees cast long shadows in the late afternoon sun, and the commotion of the town square seemed to be ringing in the background. Alex examined the vantage point, imagining what the witness might have seen and how it connected to the events that unfolded.

He crouched down, examining the terrain for any potential clues. Perhaps there were footprints, discarded items, or other evidence that could provide insight into the mysterious figure she had described. Every detail mattered, and Alex was determined to leave no stone unturned.

Intrigued by the drainage system adjacent to the cemetery park, memories of a past case involving Marcus and a discarded weapon flooded Alex's mind. The connection sparked an idea—could this drainage system hide a crucial piece of evidence in Henry's case as well?

With cautious optimism, Alex approached the grates covering the drainage openings. He scrutinized the area for any signs of disturbance or concealment. The thought of finding something relevant heightened his anticipation. It was a risk worth taking, a hunch born from his experience in dealing with criminal patterns.

Kneeling down, Alex carefully examined the edges of the grates, checking for any anomalies or loose fittings. He reached into his pocket, retrieving a flashlight to illuminate the dark recesses beneath. As the beam pierced through the openings, he glimpsed the dimly lit underground passage.

Alex's pulse quickened as his eyes locked onto a hammer-shaped object nestled at the bottom of the drain. The shadows cast by the surrounding darkness couldn't conceal the distinct contours of the tool.

With measured determination, Alex retrieved a pair of gloves from his pocket and pulled them on, preparing to delve into the confined space. Kneeling beside the drain, he carefully extended his arm, feeling the cool metal of the grates against his fingertips.

His hand wrapped around the handle as he gently pulled it out of the drain.

With nightfall approaching, he had to use his flashlight to examine the object.

It was all wood and very solid.

"A gavel," he thought to himself.

Securing the hammer-shaped object in an evidence bag, Alex felt the weight of the case intensify. The faint glow from the streetlights played on the contours of the item, revealing subtle details that could potentially unravel the mysteries hidden within Pineworth's history.

Carefully sealing the evidence bag, Alex glanced around the quiet cemetery. The shadows seemed to whisper ancient tales, and the distant hoot of an owl added an eerie soundtrack to his thoughts. The drive back to the station was a silent journey, the smoothness of the engine punctuating his contemplation.

Once at the station, Alex logged the evidence, noting the significance of this discovery. The hammer, tucked away in its transparent enclosure, now held the potential to unveil truths and expose the concealed dynamics of Pineworth's founding families.

It felt like this was a pivotal moment in the investigation, and Alex was determined to piece together the fragments of the past, no matter how dark or deeply buried.

Detective Maya greeted Alex as he entered the station, her eyes reflecting a mixture of curiosity and anticipation. The air in the room held a subtle tension, conceding the importance of the evidence Alex had just uncovered. With the evidence bag securely in hand, he approached her.

"Alex, what do you have?" Maya inquired her tone a blend of professionalism and intrigue.

"I found this in the drainage system near the cemetery," Alex explained, handing over the sealed evidence bag containing the hammer-shaped object. "It might be the missing piece we need."

Maya examined the evidence with a practiced eye, appreciating the weight of the discovery. "Good work, Alex. Let's get this to the lab for analysis. It could provide the link we've been searching for."

As they walked toward the forensic lab, a shared sense of determination permeated the atmosphere. The investigation, once a complex puzzle with missing pieces, now seemed to be converging toward a clearer picture.

In the small, dimly lit room of the police station, Detective Maya and Alex huddled over the details of the potential murder weapon – a gavel. The atmosphere was charged with the anticipation of unraveling the mystery that had haunted Pineworth.

"Why a gavel?" Maya questioned, with a questioning look on her face. "It's not something you just carry around with you."

Alex leaned back in his chair, running a hand through his hair as he pondered the possibilities. "I think the perp must have been spooked by the witness. In the process of fleeing, they might have discarded it in the drain, hoping to dispose of any evidence."

Maya nodded thoughtfully, her mind working through the implications. "Could it be a symbol? A message of some sort?"

Alex considered the idea, recognizing the layers of complexity the case was beginning to reveal.

"Wouldn't surprise me with this case," he replies.

Detective Maya glanced at Alex with a hint of approval. "Good job, Alex. You seem to have a gift for cracking these cases." She offered a brief, encouraging smile. "Go home and get some rest. I'll give you a call as soon as the results from the lab come back. You need to stay sharp for what comes next."

Alex nodded appreciatively, recognizing the weight of the investigation resting on their shoulders. "Thanks, Maya."

As Alex left the station, the night air carried a sense of anticipation. The gavel, snug in its evidence bag, held the promise of answers. Yet, it also symbolized the enigma that surrounded Pineworth's history – a mystery Alex was determined to unravel, piece by piece.

Chapter 7
The Gavel of Justice

THE SHRILL RING OF Alex's phone pierced the early morning silence, jolting him from his restless sleep. He fumbled for the device, his mind racing as he answered the call. Maya's voice, a mix of urgency and anticipation, relayed the news he had been waiting for.

"Alex, the results are in. Get to the station as soon as you can."

In an instant, weariness gave way to adrenaline. He threw on his clothes, bypassing the morning routine, and sped to the police station. The dim glow of streetlights painted fleeting shadows on the pavement as he navigated the quiet streets of Pineworth.

Upon arrival, Maya greeted him with a tight-lipped expression that betrayed the weight of the information she held.

Alex sat in his office next to Maya, the document before him like a cryptic map to Pineworth's secrets. The harsh overhead light cast an unwavering glow on the text, revealing the unsettling truth about the gavel's role in Henry's demise.

His eyes scanned the report, each word etching deeper into his consciousness. "Presence of Henry Winters' blood is confirmed. Multiple recent dents were observed on the gavel. No additional DNA detected."

Alex was hoping for just one more piece of evidence besides Henry's DNA. He knows that without any other evidence, the likelihood that they will find the killer is slim.

Silence enveloped the room as Alex absorbed the significance of the findings. The gavel, once a symbol of order and authority, now stood as a grim artifact of violence.

"Well, you have your murder weapon. What next?" Maya asks.

Alex leaned back in his chair, the weight of the investigation pressing on his shoulders.

"Now, we dig deeper. We follow the trail left by this gavel, trace it back to the hands that wielded it against Henry."

Maya replies, "Any leads on who might've used it?"

"I have my suspicions," Alex replied, his gaze fixed on the evidence. "But we need more than hunches. We need to revisit the past, unravel Pineworth's history, and see where the threads connect."

Maya sighed on the other end. "It's a tangled web, Alex. How deep are you willing to go?"

"As deep as it takes," he affirmed. "We owe it to Henry, to the truth, and to this town. The answers are here; we just need to piece them together."

"Alex, you've got a knack for this. I mean, you might have cracked the case wide open with that gavel. Impressive," Maya commended, her tone a mix of admiration and camaraderie.

He chuckled lightly, appreciating the encouragement. "Thanks, Maya. It's Pineworth, you know? Nothing is ever straightforward here."

"True. And I know it's your case, but don't forget, I'm here to help. We're a team," she reminded him.

Alex nodded. "I appreciate that. This town has a way of keeping its secrets, but we're going to get to the bottom of this."

Maya's voice held a hint of determination. "Absolutely. Let's find justice for Henry. Stay safe, Alex."

"You too, Maya. We'll get through this," he assured her.

As Detective Maya walked out of his office, Alex started to plan his next move.

There were questions that he wanted answered. Was the gavel a symbol?

Why was Henry at the Pineworth Cemetery to begin with?

Was it to meet someone? The killer?

Alex decided to pay Mrs. Winters another visit. Perhaps she could shed some light on why he was at the cemetery, to begin with.

The morning sun shines bright as Alex approaches Mrs. Winters' house. He knocked on the door, and after a moment, it creaked open, revealing the grieving widow.

"Detective Reynolds, back so soon?" she greeted, her eyes still holding the grief from the recent events.

"Yes, Mrs. Winters. I was hoping we could talk some more," Alex replied.

She stepped aside, inviting him in. The living room still held the remnants of a life intertwined with memories and family photos. Alex took a seat, and Mrs. Winters settled in a worn armchair.

"Did you find anything else?" she inquired, her voice hopeful.

"We did, actually. We found a gavel near the crime scene," Alex explained, watching her reaction closely.

Her eyes widened, a mixture of surprise and confusion. "A gavel? What on earth would that be doing there?"

"That's what I'm trying to figure out. But before we delve into that, can you tell me why your husband might have been at the cemetery that night?" Alex asked gently.

She sighed, the weight of the question evident in her eyes. "Thomas always found solace there. He loved history, and the cemetery held the stories of those who built this town. It was his way of connecting with the past."

"Did he ever mention anything specific about the cemetery or his visits there?" Alex probed.

Mrs. Winters, lost in thought, suddenly recalled another detail. "Detective Reynolds, there was something else. Right before Thomas left that night, he mentioned receiving an email. Someone claimed to have information about the founding families and wanted to meet him at the cemetery."

Alex leaned forward, his interest piqued. "Did he say who the email was from or what kind of information they had?"

She shook her head. "No, he didn't share the details with me. Thomas was always cautious, and he didn't want to raise false hopes. But it intrigued him enough to go out that night."

Alex made a mental note of the new piece of information. An unknown person is reaching out to Henry about the founding families—could this be connected to the torn-out page from the journal?

"Thank you, Mrs. Winters. If you have the email or any more details, it could be crucial for the investigation," Alex suggested.

"I'm afraid Thomas was meticulous about his privacy. He never saved personal emails on our shared computer. But I hope it helps," she replied, a hint of regret in her voice.

During the conversation with Mrs. Winters, she brought up Sgt. Thompson and his role in supporting Matthew during this challenging time.

"It's truly heartening to hear that Sgt. Thompson has been a source of comfort for Matthew," Mrs. Winters commented. "It's not easy for anyone to navigate through something like this."

Mrs. Winters smiled faintly, reminiscing about the bond between Matthew and Sgt. Thompson. "Sgt. Thompson has been a familiar figure in our lives since Matthew's school days. He was Matthew's School Resource Officer back in Crestwood, and they formed a connection early on."

"Henry always loved hearing how Matthew would come home talking about being an officer just like Sgt. Thompson one day," she continued.

Alex smiled back. He saw firsthand how James was there for Matthew. He was glad the kid had someone.

As the conversation continued, Mrs. Winters delved into the intricate threads of the Winters family, revealing another potential lead for Alex.

"You know, Alex, there's someone else in the family who shared a profound interest in our history," Mrs. Winters reflected. "Henry's little sister, Samantha. She and Henry would spend hours discussing our family's past, especially the details surrounding the town's founding. Samantha is quite knowledgeable about our history, and she might have insights that could help you understand what Henry was working on."

This revelation ignited a new possibility in the investigation.

"Do you think she would be able to speak with me today?" asked Alex.

"I will give her a call and see," replied Mrs. Winters. Just then, she stepped into the other room to make the call.

The anticipation heightened as Mrs. Winters returned from making the call to Samantha. A glimmer of hope illuminated her eyes as she shared the news with Alex.

"Samantha has agreed to meet with you," she informed him. "She suggested the coffee shop in town. It seems she's willing to share what she knows. I hope this brings some clarity to Henry's work and helps you unravel the mystery surrounding his research."

This development injected a renewed sense of purpose into Alex's investigation. The coffee shop rendezvous promised a potential breakthrough, and he couldn't help but feel a surge of determination to piece together the puzzle that Henry had left behind.

The quaint coffee shop exuded a comforting aroma of freshly brewed coffee as Alex stepped inside. The rhythmic hum of conversations and the gentle clinking of cups created a cozy ambiance. He scanned the room and spotted Samantha sitting in a corner, engrossed in a book.

Approaching her table, Alex greeted Samantha, "Hi, Samantha. I'm Detective Alex Bennett.

Your sister-in-law mentioned that you might be able to shed some light on his research."

Samantha looked up, her eyes revealing a mixture of grief and curiosity. "Yes, Detective. Henry and I often discussed our family history. He was passionate about uncovering the truth."

Alex took a seat, eager to delve into the conversation. "I appreciate you taking the time to meet with me. Anything you can share might help us understand the circumstances surrounding Henry's passing."

Samantha nodded, setting aside her book. "Henry believed there was more to our town's history than what's commonly known. He was fixated on an old journal that belonged to our grandfather, Thomas Winters. It contained details about the founding families."

Intrigued, Alex leaned forward. "Did he ever mention what specifically caught his attention in the journal?"

"He was particularly interested in one page," Samantha recalled.

As Samantha began recounting the contents of the torn-out page, a heavy silence settled in the room. Alex listened intently, realizing the weight of the revelations from the hidden journal entry.

"The page in the journal," Samantha started, her voice steady but filled with emotion, "it accused the Carters, Thompsons, and Phillips of using their influence during the town's founding.

According to Henry, they manipulated the establishment of the Phillips family as sheriffs and judges to facilitate the theft of land."

"So the Winters were not involved in this theft?" he asks.

"As far as the journal says, which is pretty biased being written by a Winters family member, we were a family trying to be the voice of reason. Although we could never compete with the money and power of the other families," she says.

The detective absorbed the shocking information, contemplating the potential ramifications of such explosive allegations.

"Did Henry share this information with anyone else, or did he mention any threats or concerns related to it?" Alex inquired, trying to grasp the full scope of Henry's discoveries.

"He mentioned bringing it up at the meeting with all the families. He said most just wrote it off as old news." Samantha states.

"Do you think this is a valid reason for someone to harm your brother?" Alex asks gently.

"Well, I am sure you have heard this before, but you never know with these families. I spend a lot of time on our history to one day tell my own kids. Even then, I am never around the other families." she replies.

Understanding the consequence of Henry's pursuit and the risks involved, Alex nodded thoughtfully. "Samantha, I appreciate your honesty. This information could be vital to understanding why your brother was targeted."

Samantha took a moment before responding, "I want to help, Detective. If there's anything I can do to assist in finding out who did this to Henry, I'm here."

"Thank you, Samantha. Your cooperation is invaluable," Alex said with gratitude. "If you remember anything else or if there's anyone else Henry might have shared this with, please let me know."

Samantha nodded, her gaze distant as if contemplating the unfolding events. The small coffee shop became a nexus of shared secrets, and Alex was determined to untangle the threads that led to Henry's tragic end.

Alex left the coffee shop and returned to the police department. Just as he sat down, Chief Brown walked in.

"Alex, what can you tell me about the gavel, and have you made any progress on the information?"

Alex leaned forward, ready to share the recent developments.

"Chief, the gavel is consistent with Henry's blood, and it shows signs of recent use. But the crucial piece of information is from Samantha Winters. According to her, the torn-out page from the journal accuses the Carters, Thompsons, and Phillips of manipulating the town's founding for their own gain."

Chief Brown's eyes widened as he processed the weight of the accusation. "That's a serious allegation."

"Would something that happened that far back really affect these people today?" Alex asks.

"These families still play a vital role. We have areas in this town that are less fortunate than others. If it comes out that the decisions of these few led to the suffering of others, it could play a huge role, especially for those that still hold prestigious roles." The chief says.

"Like Mayor Carter?" Alex questions.

"Him and also people like Ethan Phillips, who is still a judge in this town," Brown replies.

Chief Brown bid Alex farewell, his departure leaving the detective alone with the weight of the investigation pressing upon him. The door closed behind the chief, and the quietness of the police station enveloped the room.

Taking a moment to collect his thoughts, Alex glanced at the evidence board adorned with crime scene photos, witness statements, and now the revelation from Samantha Winters. The urgency of the situation settled in, and the stakes were higher than a typical murder case. The history and integrity of the town were on the line.

Afterward, Alex brought himself back to the murder weapon.

As Alex pondered the significance of the gavel, questions swirled in his mind like a relentless storm. Why a gavel? It wasn't a common choice for a murder weapon. Its presence hinted at a deliberate message, a symbolic act to underscore a deeper motive.

The detective's fingers traced the rough edges of the evidence bag containing the ominous tool. Each dent on its surface now held a story—a narrative of violence that disrupted the town's quiet facade.

Alex leans back in his chair. His hands were over his face. He wanted so badly to find the answer to all the questions he had.

Just then, Sgt. Thompson walked past his office.

Sgt. Thompson, ever observant, noticed the weight of stress etched on Alex's face as he walked past his office. Sensing the burden that came with the ongoing investigation, Thompson decided to extend an olive branch. He paused by the doorway, his expression conveying both understanding and camaraderie.

"Hey, Alex," Thompson said with a friendly tone. "I couldn't help but notice the load you're carrying. How about taking a break? I'm having a little cookout at my place later. Good food, good company—it might do you some good to refuel, especially with that case on your shoulders."

The invitation carried a genuine warmth, a gesture of solidarity from one first responder to another. Recognizing the sincerity in Thompson's eyes, Alex contemplated the offer. A break from the case, a chance to unwind in the company of friends—perhaps it was precisely what he needed.

"Thanks, James," Alex replied, a slight smile breaking through the tension on his face. "I appreciate the invite. I'll be there later tonight. A break is just what I need."

Thompson nodded in understanding, his expression conveying a silent look of understanding the challenges that came with their line of work. "Looking forward to having you there, Alex. We all need a breather now and then."

With a sense of gratitude for the camaraderie offered by his colleague, Alex returned to his work, knowing that the evening's cookout promised a welcome respite from the demands of the ongoing investigation.

AS ALEX APPROACHED James Thompson's house later that night, the savory aroma of burgers on the grill filled the air, making his stomach growl involuntarily. The warm glow of lights spilled out from the open windows, and the distant chatter of laughter and children playing signaled the lively atmosphere within.

Upon entering, he was greeted by the lively scene—a picturesque family setting. James' children raced around the yard, their laughter blending with the sizzle of meat on the grill. The inviting atmosphere immediately eased some of the tension that had been there throughout the investigation.

James, wearing a friendly grin, emerged from the backyard, extending a welcoming hand. "Alex, glad you could make it. Meet the crew!" he exclaimed, introducing Alex to his wife Ella, their daughter Ava, and son Noah.

As they engaged in friendly banter, Alex couldn't help but appreciate the sense of normalcy that the Thompson family exuded—a stark contrast to the complexities he faced in his detective role.

Shortly after Alex's arrival, the door swung open again, revealing Nathan Reynolds and Sarah. Sarah's daughter, filled with excitement, rushed to join the lively group of children already playing in the yard.

Nathan greeted Alex with a nod and a firm handshake. "Good to see you, Detective. Glad you could make it," he said, a friendly smile on his face.

The merging of the two groups—James' family and Sarah with her daughter—created a convivial atmosphere. As they exchanged stories and laughter, the cares of the day began to fade into the background, replaced by the simple joy of camaraderie. The aroma of grilling burgers and the racket of children's laughter blended seamlessly, casting a warm and comforting ambiance over the evening.

As the aroma of grilling burgers filled the air, Nathan, Alex, and James gathered around the backyard grill. The sun dipped below the horizon, casting a warm glow on the scene.

James, flipping burgers with practiced ease, couldn't resist teasing Nathan.

"So, Nathan, when are you planning to pop the big question to Sarah? Ella and I are waiting for another wedding to attend."

Nathan chuckled, shaking his head. "James, we've only been seeing each other for a few months. Let's not rush things."

Alex chimed in, "James, not everyone moves as fast as you did."

James grinned, "Fair enough. Take your time, but mark my words when you know, you know."

Nathan smiled, appreciating the friendly banter. The conversation shifted to lighter topics as they discussed work, the town's upcoming events, and the joys of grilling. The kids played in the yard, laughter all around them.

Alex turned to Nathan with a friendly smile. "So, Nathan, how's life treating you as a cop?"

Nathan took a moment to savor the atmosphere before responding. "It's been rewarding, Alex. Challenging at times, but I feel like I'm making a difference in the community. Learning a lot from Sgt. Harris, too."

Alex nodded, appreciating Nathan's dedication. "It's not an easy job, but it's good to hear you find it rewarding. Any particular moments that stand out?"

Nathan thought for a moment, recalling various incidents. "Well, there was this one time during a traffic stop. Sarge gave me some tough love and taught me a lesson about setting up right on the passenger side. It's all about safety, you know."

Alex chuckled, recognizing the importance of those lessons. "Safety first, always. It's crucial, especially in this line of work. You'll keep learning, Nathan. It never really stops."

Nathan took a sip of his drink and turned his attention to Alex. "So, how's life as a detective, Alex? I've heard it's quite different from being on patrol."

Alex leaned back, a reflective look on his face. "It has its moments, Nathan. Some days are great, and you feel like you're really making progress. Other times, it can be quite challenging, especially with cases like the current one."

James chimed in, his eyes curious. "Current case, huh? Anything you can share with us, or is it all hush-hush detective stuff?"

Alex chuckled, appreciating the camaraderie. "Well, without going into too much detail, we're dealing with this murder investigation. It's a puzzle, and we're trying to put the pieces together."

Nathan raised an eyebrow, intrigued. "Must be tough. How do you handle the pressure?"

Alex thought for a moment before responding, "You learn to manage the pressure over time. Having a supportive team and friends who understand the job helps. Plus, cookouts like these are a good way to decompress."

Nathan nodded, taking in the scene. "Yeah, these gatherings are a welcome break from the daily grind. And James, you're becoming quite the department favorite with these cookouts of yours."

James grinned, flipping a burger on the grill. "Well, good food and good company can work wonders. Plus, it's a chance for all of us to unwind a bit."

"So James, are you related to the Thompson family, which is one of the founding members of the city?"

James chuckled, shaking his head. "Nope, not that lucky. Same last name, different lineage. I wish, though; they're loaded."

Nathan chimed in, "Yeah, those founding families seem to have a lot of history, don't they?"

Alex nodded, taking a sip from his drink. The conversation shifted, providing a brief escape from the intensity of the investigation, even if just for a moment.

James noticed a shift in Alex's demeanor and decided to steer the conversation away from the investigation. "So, Alex, is there a lucky girl in your life?"

Alex looked at his drink for a moment before responding, "No, not anymore. I did have a fiancée named Chloe, but things got complicated. She didn't want to stay in Pineworth, and I couldn't imagine leaving this place, especially as a detective."

Nathan, sensing the change in tone, offered some support. "Relationships can be tough, man. It's good you're focusing on your career, though."

James smiled at Alex and added, "We make many sacrifices for the job, my friend. But one day, a day will come when someone will be willing to make that sacrifice with you."

Just then, Ella walked over and gave him a kiss on the cheek. "Come on, it's time to eat," she said with a warm smile.

The aroma of grilling burgers filled the air as they all gathered around the table, sharing laughs, stories, and a sense of camaraderie that only a close-knit community could provide. It was a welcome break for Alex, a chance to temporarily set aside the complexities of his investigation and enjoy the company of friends.

Chapter 8
Questioning the Ties

WAKING UP REFRESHED, Alex leisurely gets ready, feeling the effects of the enjoyable evening at Sergeant Thompson's cookout. The scent of coffee wafts through his kitchen, and he takes a moment to savor the quiet before the day's challenges begin. As he sips his coffee, thoughts of the ongoing investigation slowly resurface, but today feels different—more manageable. The camaraderie shared at the cookout has left a lasting sense of support.

Deciding on a fresh perspective, he heads to the police station, ready to delve into the case with renewed energy. The morning sun casts a warm glow over Pineworth, and he takes a moment to appreciate the familiar sights on his way to work. The quiet town seems to pulse with life, and for a brief moment, the weight of the investigation feels lighter.

He headed to the police station with a renewed focus, finding Maya at her desk.

Maya looked up as he approached, curious about the determined expression on his face.

"Maya, I've been thinking," Alex began. "Given the tensions we've uncovered regarding the journal and Buddy Thompson's reported anger toward Henry, I believe we should move him into the lead suspect position."

Maya paused, considering his words. "Buddy Thompson, huh? It's a bold move, Alex. What makes you think he might be involved?"

Alex leaned against her desk, explaining his reasoning. "It's all about the connections, Maya. The animosity he displayed when Henry brought up the journal at the family meeting, his prominent position in the town, and the fact that he might have something to lose if the truth about the founding families came out. It all adds up."

Maya leaned back in her chair, thoughtful. "It's a logical deduction, but we need to be careful. Accusing someone like Buddy Thompson is serious business. We need solid evidence."

"I know, Maya. That's why we're bringing him in for questioning. I believe his reactions might give us some insight. We'll tread carefully, but we can't afford to overlook anyone at this point," Alex explained.

Maya nodded. "Alright, let's go with your gut on this one. Just be prepared for anything in that room. If he's innocent, we need to figure it out quickly to avoid any unnecessary fallout."

"Agreed. We'll get to the bottom of this and bring justice to Henry's family," Alex affirmed.

Maya and Alex retreated to a quieter corner of the police station to discuss their plan of action for the upcoming interrogation with Buddy Thompson.

Maya leaned against the wall, crossing her arms. "So, what's your plan of attack, Detective?"

Alex considered the question, running through the possible scenarios in his mind. "I think I'll start out playing it safe, discussing the family history, and then gradually move into questions about his relationship with Henry and why he was so upset about the journal entry."

Maya nodded in agreement. "I think it's a solid approach. We need to gauge his reactions carefully. If he's innocent, we don't want to push too hard and create unnecessary tension. But if he's involved, we need to see if we can get him to slip up."

Alex adjusted the cuffs of his shirt, mentally preparing for the upcoming conversation. "Exactly. I want to keep the atmosphere calm initially and see if he opens up voluntarily. If there's nothing to hide, we should be able to have a straightforward conversation."

Maya added a word of caution, "But be ready to shift gears if needed. If you sense deception or evasion, don't hesitate to dig deeper. We're dealing with a potential suspect in a murder investigation, and we need to be thorough."

"Understood," Alex replied with determination. "I'll do my best to navigate the conversation smoothly while keeping our objective in mind."

Maya gave him a reassuring nod. "Good luck, Alex."

The small interrogation room felt tense as Alex entered, approaching Buddy with a nod of appreciation. "Thanks for coming in, Buddy. I appreciate your cooperation. Can I get you something to drink? Coffee, water?"

Buddy shifted in his chair. His expression was guarded but polite. "Water's fine, thanks."

Alex stepped out momentarily to fetch a bottle of water, returning to place it on the table in front of Buddy. "Hope you're comfortable. We're just here to have a conversation. No pressure."

Buddy nodded, taking a sip of water. "Sure, Detective. Happy to help however I can."

Alex settled into the chair across from Buddy, adopting a relaxed posture. "Great. First off, I wanted to talk a bit about Pineworth's history. Your family has been here for generations, right?"

Buddy nodded, "Yeah, that's right. We've been part of this town for a long time."

Alex steered the conversation toward family dynamics and the community's history, carefully leading up to the more sensitive topic. "So, you're familiar with the founding families and their roles in shaping Pineworth. It's an interesting part of our town's heritage."

Buddy responded, "Sure, it is. Our families have played a significant role in building and maintaining this place."

Alex continued, "I heard there's been some tension regarding discussions about the town's history. Particularly, there was some disagreement about a journal entry related to the founding families. Henry Winters seemed to believe there was more to the story. Do you know anything about that?"

Buddy's expression tensed slightly, but he replied cautiously, "Yeah, I heard about it. Henry had some ideas that didn't sit well with everyone. But it's just history, right? People interpret it differently."

Alex kept the tone conversational, delving deeper into the details. "Absolutely, everyone's entitled to their perspective. Did you and Henry ever discuss these differences in opinion? Any heated arguments?"

Buddy shrugged, "We might've disagreed, but nothing too heated. People get passionate about their family's history, that's all."

Alex nodded, steering the conversation toward Buddy's family history. "Running businesses for generations must have its own set of challenges. Your family's been involved in various ventures, right? Like the general store and gas stations in town. Quite a legacy."

Buddy leaned back, pride evident in his voice. "Yeah, we're proud of it. Trying to keep things going, you know? It's not always easy, but we manage."

Shifting gears, Alex brought the discussion back to recent events. "I've heard there were disagreements about Henry's research, specifically the journal entry. Did he ever share with you what he found or why it bothered him so much?"

Buddy sighed, his shoulders tensing slightly. "Not really. Henry liked to stir things up, questioning the status quo. But he never went into specifics. Just said there was more to the story than what people thought."

Intrigued, Alex continued, "And how did that make you feel? His claims about the founding families, did they bother you?"

Buddy's expression tightened, but he responded carefully, "It's always tough when someone questions your family's history. But it's just talk, right? People have different opinions."

Alex leaned back, maintaining a friendly demeanor. "Absolutely, Buddy. Opinions make the world interesting. Now, as a store owner, you must interact with a lot of people. Did you have any customers or employees who might have mentioned something unusual on the day Henry was found in the cemetery?"

Buddy shook his head, "No, Detective. The store was busy as usual. I didn't hear anything about Henry that day."

Alex's demeanor shifted, adopting a more serious tone. "Buddy, you have a shop in town, about 500 yards away from the scene. You're telling me you didn't hear or see anything unusual that day?"

Buddy's response was swift, "No, Detective. It was a regular day at the store. I didn't notice anything out of the ordinary."

Alex leaned forward, his gaze focused. "You see, Buddy, we've got witnesses who claimed they saw someone near the cemetery that day. Someone who seemed agitated. Someone who might have been involved in what happened to Henry. You wouldn't happen to know anything about that, would you?"

Buddy shifted uncomfortably in his chair. "Detective, I'm telling you the truth. I didn't see or hear anything. I'm just as surprised as anyone about what happened to Henry."

Alex leaned in, his eyes focused on Buddy, "You're the youngest of the heads of the founding family, right? That's a considerable responsibility for a 32-year-old. Did you ever feel like what Henry said in the journal put pressure on you? Like you had to protect something you recently inherited?"

Buddy's expression tightened, but he maintained his composure. "Look, Detective, I might be young, but I can handle the family business just fine. I didn't need Henry or anyone else telling me what to do. And I certainly wouldn't resort to violence because of some accusations."

Alex studied Buddy's reactions, searching for any subtle signs of discomfort or deception.

Alex, his gaze unwavering, brought up the issue of land ownership. "Buddy, I looked into the history of the land your general store and gas station sit on. It seems there was a lopsided deal, taking land from the Winters and giving it to the Thompsons. Was this the cause of the disagreement?"

Buddy's expression tightened further, but he maintained his composure. "Detective, that's just an accusation. It frustrates me, yes, but I wouldn't resort to hurting Henry just because he believed it."

Alex leaned back, absorbing Buddy's response.

"Alright, Buddy. I appreciate your honesty. We're just trying to piece together what happened, and your cooperation is crucial. If anything comes to mind, don't hesitate to reach out."

As Buddy left the room, Alex remained thoughtful, contemplating the dynamics of the Thompson family and the possible motivations behind Henry's accusations in the journal.

After Buddy left the interrogation room, Alex rejoined Maya in the observation area.

Alex sighed, "Buddy was definitely angry at Henry. He didn't hold back about his frustration with the accusations in the journal. However, I'm not entirely convinced that he was angry enough to harm him. He seemed genuine, no indicators that he was hiding anything."

Maya studied Alex's face, and curiosity etched across her features. "If not Buddy, then who else could be a suspect?"

Alex sighed, his mind churning with possibilities. "I'm not entirely certain, Maya. I might need to rethink my strategy. Buddy seemed angry at Henry, but he may not have acted on it."

Maya observed the frustration on Alex's face. "You seem stuck," she remarked, concerned in her voice. "Maybe we should go back over the known evidence. We might find a detail we've missed or a connection we haven't considered."

Alex looked up, contemplating her words. "You might be onto something. A fresh look at the evidence could reveal a new angle or lead."

They gathered the case files, spreading them across the desk. The crime scene photos, witness statements, and forensic reports became their focus.

The small interrogation room felt confined as Alex recounted the evidence to Maya. The weight of the case hung in the air, and he needed to share his thoughts.

"YOU KNOW, MAYA, WE'VE got the cemetery, the gavel, the journal, and that torn-out page. I'm just not putting it all together right. It's like I'm missing a piece of the puzzle, and I can't figure out where it fits," Alex admitted, frustration evident in his voice.

Maya chuckled as they left the interrogation room, her voice ringing down the narrow hallway. "You know, Alex, sometimes I wish solving a case was as easy as judging a bake-off contest. Clear criteria, a set of rules, and a sweet reward at the end."

Alex cracked a small smile, appreciating the levity in Maya's comment. "Yeah, that would make life simpler, wouldn't it? But alas, we deal with the messier stuff – human nature, motives, and the unexpected twists."

Alex's eyes lit up with sudden realization. "Maya, I might have something. Keep the word 'judge' in mind."

With those cryptic words, he briskly led the way toward the cemetery, the crunch of gravel beneath their shoes the only break in the still night. The wrought-iron gate greeted them with a rusty groan as they entered, the sunlight through the trees casting long shadows over the silent tombstones.

Maya followed, curiosity etched across her features. "What are we looking for?"

"The judge," Alex muttered, his gaze scanning the surroundings. "Henry's obsession with the founding families might be connected to an actual judge, a key figure from the past."

Maya gave a surprised look. "A judge? Like, an individual?"

"Exactly," Alex replied, his voice tinged with anticipation. "We've been focused on families, businesses, and land. But what if there's a person, a judge, who played a crucial role back then? Someone who could tie everything together."

As they ventured deeper into the cemetery, gravestones stood as silent witnesses to the passage of time.

Maya squinted against the sunlight, looking at Alex with a quizzical expression.

"So, Alex," Maya began, shielding her eyes from the sun, "what are we looking for here?

"So this is the very spot Henry was lying when Nathan pulled up." He said. "Notice anything about the tombstone there?" He continued.

"It says Johnathan Phillips. Do you know who that is?" Maya responded.

"Remember the land agreement I found with Mr. Beal at the History Museum? The one between the Winters and the Carters?" he replied.

Maya nodded, recalling the document they had discussed earlier.

"Well, the name Jonathan Phillips was on that paperwork. He was one of the signatories in the land agreement between the founding families," Alex explained. "It got me thinking—why would a judge be involved in a land deal like that? There's more to this than meets the eye."

Maya's eyes widened with realization. "So, we're connecting Judge Jonathan Phillips, Pineworth's first, to the founding families' disputes over land. Do you think this has something to do with Henry's murder?"

"It's a possibility," Alex replied, his mind racing with the newfound connection. "If I can uncover what happened back then, I might find the motive behind Henry's death."

Alex headed back to the history museum to meet with Mr. Beal. The sun hung low in the sky, casting a blue and pink glow over Pineworth. As he entered the historical records room, Alex greeted Mr. Beal, who was meticulously organizing documents.

"Good afternoon, Mr. Beal. I need to take another look at that land agreement between the Winters and the Carters," Alex requested.

"Of course, Detective Bennett. It's right here," Mr. Beal replied, retrieving the aged document from a nearby shelf.

As Alex carefully examined the land agreement, he focused on the details related to Judge Jonathan Phillips. The intricate web of connections between the founding families and the involvement of a judge intrigued him.

"Mr. Beal, do you have any additional information on Judge Jonathan Phillips? Anything that might shed light on his role in this land deal?" Alex inquired.

Mr. Beal thought for a moment before recalling, "Well, there might be more information in the town's archives. I can guide you there if you'd like."

"Thank you, Mr. Beal. That would be incredibly helpful," Alex said, appreciating the archivist's assistance.

As Alex delved into the historical archives, he unearthed a trove of information about Judge Jonathan Phillips. The old articles painted a picture of a man who strongly favored the founding families, particularly the Thompsons. One particular incident caught Alex's attention – a case involving a Thompson accused of theft of cattle.

In the faded print of a newspaper from decades ago, the story unfolded. The people of the day were outraged as Judge Phillips had seemingly allowed a Thompson family member to go free despite compelling evidence of cattle theft. The articles hinted at connections and influence that swayed the scales of justice in favor of the influential families.

Alex couldn't help but draw parallels between this historical incident and the current dynamics in Pineworth. The stories of the past seemed to resonate in the present, raising questions about the influence these founding families held over the town and its legal system.

Alex arrives at the police department with a sense of urgency. He seeks out Chief Brown to discuss a critical development in the case. Entering Chief Brown's office, he finds him engrossed in paperwork.

"Chief," Alex begins, "I've come across some information that might shed light on the motive behind Henry Winters' murder. It involves Judge Jonathan Phillips, one of the founding figures of Pineworth."

Chief Brown looks up, intrigued. "Go on, Alex. What did you find?"

Alex proceeds to share the historical details about Judge Phillips and his apparent bias toward the founding families, particularly the Thompsons. He explains the incident involving a Thompson accused of cattle theft, emphasizing the perceived favoritism that allowed the individual to escape conviction.

"Considering this historical context and its potential connection to Henry's investigation, I think it's crucial to question the current Judge Phillips. His influence might have played a role in shaping the town's history, and we need to know if there's any truth to Henry's claims," Alex states.

Chief Brown nods thoughtfully. "Alright, Alex. I'll arrange for the interrogation. This is a delicate matter, but if it leads us to the truth, we need to pursue it. Keep me updated on any developments."

With Chief Brown's support, Alex feels a renewed sense of determination. The pieces of the puzzle are slowly falling into place, and the investigation takes another crucial turn.

Chapter 9
A Judge's Dilemma

AS HE SETTLED INTO his office, Maya entered, a determined expression on her face.

"Alex, Judge Phillips is in the interrogation room, waiting for you," Maya informed him, her tone conveying the urgency of the situation.

Alex nodded, ready for the upcoming conversation. He stood up, adjusting his jacket, and made his way to the interrogation room. The door swung open, revealing Judge Phillips seated calmly inside. The judge's steely gaze met Alex's, a silence in the room showing the weight of their impending discussion.

"Judge Phillips, thank you for joining us today," Alex began, his voice measured.

The judge nodded in response, an air of quiet confidence surrounding him. Alex took a seat across from the elderly man, Maya observing from the corner of the room. The atmosphere was charged with anticipation as Alex delved into the matters at hand.

"We've been delving into the history of Pineworth, particularly its founding families. Your family's name surfaces prominently, especially concerning the early agreements that shaped the town," Alex explained, choosing his words carefully.

The judge listened attentively, his demeanor unchanged, as if he were an ancient guardian of the town's secrets.

"We came across documents outlining a land agreement involving the Carters, the Thompsons, and the Phillips—your family," Alex continued, studying the judge's reactions.

Judge Phillips defended the historical context, "Those were different times, Detective. The town needed structure, and such agreements were necessary."

In the following conversation with Judge Phillips, Alex skillfully navigated through the layers of Pineworth's history, probing for any connections that could shed light on Henry Winters' murder.

Phillips, seated across from him, appeared stoic, and Alex sensed there was more to the story.

"Judge," Alex began, "I spoke with you not too long ago. I mentioned Henry's journal and its contents, but you downplayed its significance. Do you share your own perspective?"

Phillips maintained his calm demeanor, his eyes meeting Alex's with an air of wisdom.

"Detective, please call me Ethan. Every family has its secrets. Some stories are better left in the past. I might believe that revealing the contents of the journal would only stir unnecessary trouble."

Alex leaned forward, his curiosity undeterred. "But if the journal holds clues about the town's founding, it could be crucial to our investigation. We need to understand its significance."

"You, a judge of all people, know this." He continued.

"You are right. I just didn't think this would be an issue. Yes, my family has been judges here in Pineworth for as long as this town has been. Henry did bring his journal. He wanted to put our ancestors for what they did. He said we should right all the wrongs they did." Ethan replied.

"As you can imagine, most of us did not think so. We have benefited from the privilege we were born into. We also rely on the people of this town to keep our position. If they think we are still running a scheme, they would be looking to replace us. We have our name to live up to." He continued.

"So the journal said the things that would harm people in high places?" Alex questioned.

"The journal, a specific page in it, held an account that was true. They took a lot of land from other people. Even some from the Winters. Some we still hold. Others that were sold off to gain our families' wealth." Ethan said.

"That being said, no one from my family did Henry any harm. We were all on vacation at the beach. We go every year around this time. I will send you the receipts for an alibi if you wish." He continued.

Alex nodded appreciatively, "Thank you for your cooperation, Judge Phillips. If we have any further questions, we'll be in touch."

As Judge Phillips left the room, mentioning the event for Mayor Carter's reelection, Alex's mind raced. He decided to attend the event, suspecting it could provide additional insights or connections to the ongoing investigation.

The night air was alive with anticipation as Alex arrived at the venue hosting Mayor Carter's reelection event. A canopy of twinkling lights adorned the entrance, casting a warm glow over the scene. The conversation and distant music created an atmosphere of festivity.

Alex parked his car discreetly and blended into the arriving crowd, the allure of laughter and clinking glasses filling the air. As he approached the entrance, he noticed the vibrant campaign banners declaring "Reelect Mayor Carter" waving in the breeze. The scent of freshly cut grass and blooming flowers added to the sense of occasion.

Adjusting his tie and straightening his jacket, Alex entered the venue, determined to navigate the political landscape with a detective's intuition.

As Alex mingled through the crowd, he spotted the Mayor's brother, Michael Carter, engaged in conversation with a group of supporters. Approaching with a spiked interest, Alex joined the conversation about the upcoming election.

Michael exuded an air of confidence, but beneath the surface, there was a subtle tension. As they discussed the mayoral race, Michael leaned in and confided, "You know, Alex, this is one of the first times in Pineworth's history that a Carter is coming close to losing an election. It's a tough battle this time around."

Curious about the sentiment for change, Alex probed further, "Why do you think there's a call for change, Michael?"

Michael took a thoughtful pause before responding, "Pineworth is evolving, Alex. People want different things, and there's a growing sense that we need to adapt to the times. But don't get me wrong, I firmly believe my brother is the best candidate for the job. It's just the way things are right now. Who knows, maybe one day I'll throw my hat in the ring when he decides to step down."

Michael turned to Alex, genuine concern etched on his face. "Alex, I've been following the news about that terrible incident. I truly hope you catch whoever did it. Pineworth needs justice, and we can't have someone going around hurting others."

Alex nodded appreciatively, recognizing the sincerity in Michael's words. Sensing there might be more to uncover about the town's dynamics, he decided to explore the subject further. "It's a tough case, Michael. Do you have any thoughts on what might have happened, or maybe any insights into Henry's connections within the community?"

Michael nodded. "Yeah, Henry and Beal were thick as thieves when it came to town history. Always digging into old records, journals, and such. You might want to check there if you haven't already."

"Thanks, Michael. I appreciate your input. If you think of anything else or hear any whispers around town, feel free to give me a call."

Michael patted Alex on the back. "Will do, Detective. Good luck with the case. And hey, don't be a stranger – swing by the office sometime. I could use a break from all this election buzz."

As Alex walked away from Michael, he couldn't shake the feeling that Michael Carter was different from the other members of the founding families. There was a laid-back quality about him, a contrast to the inherent tension and competition that seemed to permeate the relationships among the town's elite.

Alex pondered on whether Michael's demeanor was a facade or a genuine departure from the usual dynamics. Whatever the case, he filed away this observation for future consideration.

Alex's phone rang, and he saw Maya's name on the caller ID. Curious, he answered, "Hello?"

"Hey, Alex. How about a coffee at the shop? Need to discuss something," Maya suggested.

"Sure, Maya. I'll meet you there in a bit," Alex agreed, the intrigue evident in his voice.

They exchanged a few more pleasantries before hanging up. Alex, now fueled by a renewed sense of curiosity, headed to the coffee shop to catch up with Maya.

Alex arrived at the coffee shop, a quaint place nestled in the heart of town. The bell chimed as he entered, and he spotted Maya already sitting at a corner table, a cup of steaming coffee in front of her.

"Hey, Alex. Grab a seat," Maya greeted him, gesturing to the empty chair across from her.

"Thanks," Alex replied, taking a seat. He couldn't help but wonder what had prompted Maya to suggest this meeting. "What's on your mind?"

Maya sipped her coffee, breaking the momentary silence. "You know, Alex, sometimes I wish we could escape the world of law enforcement for a while. It gets overwhelming, doesn't it?"

Alex nodded, setting down his cup. "Absolutely. I often find myself needing a break, too. The job can consume you if you let it."

Maya looked around, her eyes momentarily distant. "I don't have many friends outside of the force. It's hard to explain what we go through to someone who hasn't lived it."

"Tell me about it," Alex replied, leaning back in his chair. "But hey, that's what we're here for, right? To unwind a bit and talk about something other than crime scenes and investigations."

Maya's shoulders visibly relaxed, appreciating the understanding. "Exactly. So, what's on your mind outside of the detective world?"

Alex took a much-needed sip of his coffee before responding, "You know, Maya, seeing James and Ella at the cookout the other night got me thinking. Maybe it's time for me to dip my toes back into the dating pool. They seem happy, and it made me realize that it's possible to balance personal life with the job."

Maya looked at him with a hint of a smile playing on her lips. "Dating, huh? Any particular reason you're thinking about it now?"

Alex shrugged, a little blush touching his cheeks. "Just a gut feeling, I guess. Life's too short to let it pass by without trying to find a little happiness outside of the job, don't you think?"

Maya chuckled, "Well, it's about time, Alex. I've been wondering when you'd come to that realization. Any prospects in mind, or are you diving into the unknown?"

Alex smirked, "No prospects yet. I'll figure it out as I go. But it's a start, right?"

Maya clinked her coffee cup against his, "Here's to new beginnings, my friend. And who knows, maybe you'll find someone who can handle the complexities of a detective's life."

"What about you? Anyone special?"

Maya leaned back in her chair, a wondering expression on her face. "Well, you know how it is. The job keeps me occupied. I do not have much time for a personal life, but I guess that comes with the territory. I've got a few close friends, but it's not the same as having someone to share your life with."

Alex nodded in understanding. "Yeah, I get that. It's tough to find that balance, especially in our line of work. But hey, we're not robots. We deserve a bit of happiness outside the precinct, don't we?"

Maya smiled a genuine warmth in her eyes. "Absolutely, Alex. And I hope you find what you're looking for. As for me, Imma keeps chugging along, solving cases, and maybe, just maybe, one day, I'll stumble upon something more than evidence and crime scenes."

As the conversation between Alex and Maya continued, Alex couldn't shake the subtle shift in his feelings. It wasn't just about friendship; there was something more beneath the surface. He pondered the possibility that Maya could be the person he was looking for, someone to share his life and experiences.

Yet, uncertainty hung in the air. Was he misinterpreting his emotions, or was this the beginning of something beyond friendship? Alex chose to keep these thoughts to himself for now, wanting to explore the connection they were building without jumping to conclusions.

As the moment unfolded, they continued to talk, laugh, and share stories, finding solace in each other's company. The case, which had dominated their thoughts, took a temporary backseat to the simple joys of a genuine connection between two individuals navigating the complexities of life and law enforcement.

As the evening comes to a close, Maya mentioned that duty calls early the next morning, signaling the end of their time together. Alex, knowing how close she lives to the coffee shop, offers to walk her home.

Maya playfully responded, teasing him about protecting her from potential robbers. Alex, quick on his feet, retorted with a grin, "Oh no, I have to protect robbers from you."

They stroll down the quiet street, their banter ringing in the night. The connection between them seemed to deepen, and the unspoken feelings stayed in the air as they shared a lighthearted moment, finding comfort in each other's presence. The night held the promise of something more, a connection that went beyond the bounds of duty and investigation.

Chapter 10
Cracks in the Silence

THE NEW DAY UNFOLDS with a different vibe for Alex as he prepares to tackle the challenges ahead. There's an underlying sense of optimism fueled by the anticipation of progress in the case. What makes the day even more promising is the certainty that he'll get to see Maya, a bright spot in the midst of the ongoing investigation.

Back in his familiar office Alex is immersed in reviewing the evidence in his office when Maya walks in. He can't help but feel a sense of joy as she enters the room, her presence a welcome break from the intensity of the case.

Maya flashed a warm smile as she took a seat across from Alex. "So, what puzzle do you have to share today?"

Alex leaned back in his chair, contemplating the complexities of the case. "Well, I thought the gavel was some kind of symbol, but the interview with the judge gave me nothing. Buddy Thompson sure was angry at Henry, but no evidence links him to the murder."

Maya nodded thoughtfully. "It's like we're circling around the truth, but we haven't quite hit the bullseye."

A spark of realization ignited in Alex's eyes. "Wait, I've been focusing on the wrong symbols. The gavel. It's not a symbol for the judge; it's a symbol for something else. A decision. A decision was made that night."

Maya leaned forward, intrigued. "A decision that people benefited from."

Alex rubbed his chin, deep in thought. "If Henry had revealed something that could tarnish the reputation of one of the founding families, then the person who benefits the most from his silence would be someone within those families. But it's not just about protecting a family legacy; it's about maintaining control and influence in Pineworth."

Maya leaned in, her eyes narrowing in concentration. "So, who in those families stands to lose the most if the truth comes out?"

"Let's look at their positions and influence in the town," Alex suggested. "We're not just dealing with personal reputations here; it's about power, connections, and the ability to shape the town's narrative. If the truth undermines that, it could have far-reaching consequences."

Maya nodded, absorbing the implications. "So, our suspect might not just be someone angry at Henry personally but someone safeguarding the status quo of their family and the town. We need to dig deeper into their motives and connections."

Alex continues, considering the implications. "Let's start with the Phillips. A judge's reputation is everything. If Judge Phillips is hiding something that could tarnish his image, it would make sense for him to want Henry silenced.

"And the Thompsons?" Maya asks.

Alex leaned forward, a glint of determination in his eyes. "If Henry's revelations had come to light, it could have had a significant impact on their businesses. People might avoid their stores and gas stations, affecting their financial standing and reputation in the community."

"What about the Carters? Pineworth's favorite family." She joked.

Alex pondered the implications regarding the Carters. "The Carters are in the middle of a tight election. If Henry's findings were made public, it might sway voters against them. Losing an election could have severe consequences for their family's influence and political standing in Pineworth."

Maya nodded, understanding the potential impact on the Carters.

"Well, I'm off to a theft investigation. Apparently, the Pineworth History Museum had some items taken." She says.

"Alright, let me know if you need anything," Alex responds.

With Maya leaving the room, Alex contemplated his next move. Revisiting the witness seemed like a prudent step. Perhaps she had remembered or noticed something since the day of the murder that could shed light on the case. Gathering his belongings, he headed out of the office, determined to pursue this lead and get him ever closer to solving Henry's case.

Alex Bennett stood on the doorstep of Ms. Winston's house, a sense of determination etched on his face. He raised his hand to knock, and the door creaked open slowly, revealing Ms. Winston on the other side. Recognition flickered in her eyes as she greeted him.

"Detective Bennett, isn't it?" she asked, stepping back to let him in. "What brings you back here today?"

"Ms. Winston, thank you for having me," Alex replied, his tone polite yet focused. "I wanted to follow up and see if anything has come to mind since the last time we spoke about what happened in the graveyard."

Ms. Winston paused, her expression reflecting the effort to recall details from that fateful day.

"I don't know Detective. I have been trying my best not to think about that day," she responds.

"I am sorry to bring this up again. I am just making sure we have all our bases covered." he countered.

Ms. Winston hesitated for a moment before saying, "I understand, Detective. There is something that keeps coming to me, and I believe something came to me yesterday. The man by the tree was wearing a blue hoodie with a red hat. There was some writing on the hat, but I couldn't make out what it said. He was quite far away."

Alex's eyes narrowed slightly as he processed the information. "A blue hoodie with a red hat with big writing?" he repeated.

"That's helpful, Ms. Winston. Anything specific about the wording, even if it's a vague recollection?"

Ms. Winston tapped her foot on the floor, deep in thought. "I'm sorry, Detective, it was too far to make out. But I hope it helps."

"It does," Alex assured her. "Every detail counts. If anything else comes to mind, please don't hesitate to reach out. Your cooperation is crucial to solving this case. Thank you for sharing this with me."

As Alex left Ms. Winston's home, his mind was still processing the new information about the blue hoodie and red hat. Just as he got into his car, his phone buzzed with a text message from Maya: "Get to the history museum ASAP."

A sense of urgency washed over him as he hurriedly made his way to the history museum. The possibilities raced through his mind. What had Maya discovered that required immediate attention?

As Alex arrived at the museum, he found Maya and Mr. Beal waiting for him with an intriguing smile on her face. "You'll never guess what was taken from the museum just the night before the murder," Maya said, her excitement palpable.

Curious, Alex asks. "What? What was taken?"

"A gavel!" Maya exclaimed, revealing the unexpected connection between the stolen museum artifact and the murder weapon. The revelation hit Alex with a wave of realization.

"A gavel? The same type that was used to kill Henry?" he asked, trying to grasp the significance of the discovery.

Yes, the same one," Maya confirmed. Alex immediately shifted into detective mode. "We need to check for prints. Are there any cameras set up?"

Maya nodded. "Yes, there are security cameras throughout the museum. Let's head to the surveillance room and see if we can find any footage of the break-in."

Mr. Beal took them to the security room and then told them he would be in the archive room, making sure nothing was stolen.

They quickly made their way to the surveillance room, where Maya pulled up the footage from the night of the break-in. As they watched the recording, they observed a shadowy figure sneaking into the museum, carefully avoiding detection.

Alex squinted at the screen, attempting to get a clearer view. "Enhance the image. I want to see if we can identify the person."

Maya worked her magic with the controls, zooming in on the mysterious intruder. The figure wore a hooded jacket and a hat, making it challenging to discern facial features. But there was something distinctive about the way they moved.

"We might not have a clear view of their face, but we can analyze their gait and height. It could help us narrow down potential suspects," Alex suggested.

As they continued analyzing the enhanced footage, Alex's eyes widened with recognition. "That's him!" he exclaimed, pointing at the screen. "The man was wearing a blue hoodie and red hat. The same description Ms. Winston provided for the person she saw near the crime scene."

As they continued reviewing the footage, Alex focused on the details of the person's clothing. "Pause right there," he instructed, pointing at the screen. "Enhance the view on the hat."

Maya adjusted the settings, zooming in on the hat the person was wearing. As the image became clearer, the words "Carter for Mayor" in big letters became visible.

"Mayor Carter's campaign slogan," Alex muttered, his thoughts racing.

Alex quickly snapped a picture of the man from the security footage on the museum's camera using his phone. The image captured the suspect in his blue hoodie with the "Carter for Mayor" hat. Alex then hurriedly made his way to the archives, eager to share this newfound lead with Mr. Beal.

As he entered the archives, Mr. Beal looked up from his desk, curious about the urgency in Alex's demeanor. Without wasting a moment, Alex showed him the picture on his phone.

"Mr. Beal," he said, "do you recognize this man? He was caught on camera at the museum the night it was broken into."

Mr. Beal studied the image, scratching his head in concentration. "Hmm, I can't say I know him personally, but he looks somewhat familiar. Maybe a local resident."

Alex carefully examined the broken window at the history museum, tracing the path the intruder might have taken during the break-in. As he studied the shards of glass and the torn fabric, a revelation struck him.

"Maya," he called, "look at this. The glass tore the intruder's jacket as he was getting in. If we can find the jacket, we might have a direct link to the suspect."

Maya joined him, her eyes following the torn fabric on the window frame. "Good catch, Alex. Let's gather this evidence. If we can match the torn fabric with a jacket, we'll have a solid lead on our suspect."

They carefully collected the torn fabric, preserving it as potential key evidence. With the newfound clues, they headed back to the police station to process the torn fabric and the image of the suspect in the hope of unraveling the mysteries surrounding Henry's murder.

Back at the police station, Alex and Maya sat huddled over the evidence they had gathered from the history museum. The torn fabric, the image of the suspect in the blue hoodie and red hat, and the details about the stolen gavel were all pieces of a puzzle that seemed to be slowly coming together.

Alex, with a determined expression, studied the torn fabric. "If we can identify the owner of this jacket, we might have a direct connection to the murder."

Alex leaned back in his chair, contemplating the events of the day.

Maya chuckles and says, "Well, it looks like this case was all for me to solve!"

Alex laughs and replies, "I guess so. Next time, the case is all yours."

The exchange of playful banter provided a momentary escape from the weight of the murder investigation, showcasing the camaraderie developing between them beyond the confines of their professional roles.

Alex decides to head down to the mayor's office to inquire about the person in the video. He figures Mayor Carter might recognize the individual wearing the "Carter for Mayor" hat. As he makes his way through the police station, thoughts about the potential breakthrough swirl in his mind. This new lead could be the key to solving the mystery surrounding Henry's murder.

Upon reaching the mayor's office, Alex knocks on the door before entering. Mayor Carter looks up from his desk, a curious expression on his face. "Detective Bennett, what can I do for you?" he asks.

Alex explains the recent developments, detailing the break-in at the history museum and the discovery of the stolen gavel. "We have surveillance footage of the suspect, and he was wearing a hat with your campaign slogan. Do you recognize this person?" Alex shows Mayor Carter the still image captured from the video.

The mayor studies the image for a moment, his eyes determined. "I'm sorry, Detective, but I don't recognize this person. The hat might be a campaign merchandise; anyone could have gotten hold of it. I've seen many people wearing similar ones around town. Also, his face is hidden very well."

"Thank you, Mayor Carter. I appreciate your cooperation," Alex replies with a nod. As he leaves the mayor's office, he can't help but consider the implications of the stolen gavel being linked to the campaign. It adds a layer of complexity to an already intricate case.

Alex finishes his day by putting all his new evidence in his case file. Creating a new and fresh storyline that wasn't previously there.

Although he has made strides in solving the case, he can't help feeling the urgency.

As he was getting ready to leave his office, James walked in with a grin, "Hey, Alex! Got some exciting news. We're throwing a surprise birthday party for Sarah tonight at the park, and guess what? Nathan's planning to pop the question, too. He wanted me to ask if you would be there?"

Alex, appreciating the invitation, nods, "Absolutely, James. I'll be there. Thinking of bringing Maya along, hope that's cool?"

James laughs, "Of course! The more, the merrier. It's going to be a great night."

As James walks away, Alex sees Maya in her office packing up her things for the day. He walks over and knocks on her open door.

"What's up?" she asks.

"I was wondering if you would like to come with me to a surprise birthday party for Sarah tonight? Nathan's planning to propose to her, and it should be a good time."

Maya smiles, "Sure, Alex. I'd love to go. It sounds like a fun evening."

"Great!" Alex says with a grin. "I'll swing by your place to pick you up. See you later!"

Alex parked his car outside Maya's home and waited for her to join him. When she stepped out, he couldn't help but notice the change from her usual professional attire.

Maya caught his glance and smirked, "What were you expecting, Detective? The jeans and gun combo?"

Alex grinned, "Well, not exactly, but you do clean up nicely. Ready for a night of surprises?"

Maya chuckled, "Surprises are part of the job, right?"

They left, headed towards James' home. The ride was full of talk about the investigation. They may be going to celebrate, but the case was on their mind.

They arrived at the park and waited for Nathan and Sarah to show up. The park was lined with tall, bright lights along a walking path.

James had brought Lizzy with him. She seemed especially excited.

A few minutes went by, and Nathan's silver pickup truck pulled into the park. Sarah got out of the passenger side to the loud roars of "surprise."

She seemed happily surprised.

Just then, Nathan said he had one thing to say before we all got celebrating.

"It was in this very park that I fell for you. When I needed a friend the most, you were there for me. Now, I want to be there for you and Lizzy for the rest of our lives. Will you marry me?"

She smiled with happy tears forming in her eyes.

"Yes!" she says loudly.

Everyone there cheered as Lizzy ran and gave the newly engaged couple a hug.

They looked so happy. It was a sign that things are not always so bad in this profession. Alex looked at Maya, and they shared a smile.

Chapter 11
Closing In

ALEX WALKED THROUGH the quiet graveyard at night. The shadows looked like ghosts on the tombstones under the moonlight. His shoes made a crunching sound against the gravel that filled the silence.

He wandered between the rows of tombstones, each one marking time's passing. He felt an urge to visit a specific grave. The tall, old headstone's writing was hidden in the mist. Feeling intrigued, Alex approached the headstone, his breath visible in the cold air.

Alex progressed towards the tombstone. It read, "Johnathan Phillips, Pineworth's First Judge." An eerie feeling started creeping over Alex. He paused, sensing the town's past pressuring him.

From far came a soft sound. The environment was brimming with unease. Alex saw a shadow figure in his peripheral. It was blurred as the cemetery's darkness enshrouded it.

The shadowy figure gestured. Alex felt a sudden shiver. He was mysteriously drawn nearer. The wind carried ghostly whispers, unclear yet creepy.

It was as if the very essence of Pineworth's secrets resonated in the night air.

Suddenly, the dreamlike trance shattered, and Alex awoke, drenched in a cold sweat. The ethereal atmosphere of the cemetery dissipated, leaving only the residue of an enigmatic encounter.

After rising from his bed, he goes to his kitchen to get a glass of cool water.

The cold glass of water felt refreshing against Alex's parched throat as he stood in the dimly lit kitchen, still haunted by his unsettling dream. Droplets of condensation clung to the sides of the glass, reflecting the ambient glow from the refrigerator's soft light.

Each gulp of refreshing water seemed to ease the leftover feelings of the dream, but it couldn't answer the puzzling thoughts stuck in his mind as Henry's shadowed face blended with the mystery figure from the graveyard. Real life and dream life started to overlap. This left Alex wrestling with the slipping grasp of reality.

Placing the glass aside, Alex rested against the kitchen's surface, trapped in deep thought. "Are you him, Henry?" he questioned under his breath, his quiet voice echoing in the silent house. The burden of the unresolved mystery rested heavily on him as uncertainty shaded the way forward.

Alex pondered over the importance of the dream's symbolism.

The shadow figure represented more than a mere specter; it embodied the elusive nature of the investigation. The killer's identity remained obscured, and the dream offered no concrete answers.

As his words dissipated into the quietude of the night, Alex sighed, realizing that the pursuit of truth often led through winding, shadowed paths. With a resolute determination, he decided to face the challenges that lay ahead, both in the waking world and the realm of dreams. The answers, he hoped, were waiting to be unveiled, even if they lurked in the shadows.

The quiet hum of the night persisted as Alex, unable to find solace in sleep, resigned himself to the stillness of the predawn hours. The looming day ahead demanded his attention, and he knew the responsibilities that awaited would require his utmost focus.

Moving through the familiar rituals of preparation, Alex found a peculiar comfort in the solitude of his pre-dawn routine. The soft glow of the bathroom light cast shadows across his features as he meticulously groomed, the mirror reflecting the weariness etched into his expression. The worn edges of his detective's badge caught the light, a tangible symbol of the challenges he faced.

In the dim kitchen, he brewed a strong cup of coffee, the rich aroma permeating the air and grounding him in the present. The predawn hours held a certain clarity, a silence that allowed for introspection before the clamor of the day enveloped him.

As he dressed in the familiar attire of a detective, the weight of the pending tasks settled upon his shoulders. The anticipation of a demanding day stayed in the air, yet there was a sense of purpose in the quietude of the early morning.

While the long night of wakefulness would inevitably take its toll later, Alex couldn't deny the strange allure of these moments before dawn. There was a serenity in the routine, a stillness that allowed him to gather his thoughts and brace himself for whatever challenges lay ahead.

The city, shrouded in darkness, seemed to hold its breath, as if waiting for the day to unfold.

With a final glance at himself in the mirror, Alex took a deep breath, ready to face the day that awaited him—a day that promised to bring answers, revelations, and perhaps a step closer to untangling the web of mysteries that gripped Pineworth.

The morning sun began to cast its golden hues upon Pineworth as Alex arrived at the police station. Surprisingly, Maya, usually the early riser, was already present. The synchronized entrance was an unusual occurrence, and Maya, noticing the coincidence, approached Alex.

"Morning, Alex," Maya greeted him, a curious expression on her face. "Mind if we have a quick chat?"

"Sure, Maya. What's on your mind?" Alex replied, a hint of curiosity in his voice as he followed her into a more private area.

Maya took a deep breath, her eyes meeting Alex's with a mix of sincerity and vulnerability. "Alex, here's the thing. I like you. Like, I really like you. We've had some great times together since our talk at the coffee shop, and I can sense where this is leading. I just want you to know I love this job, and it comes first. But I'm willing to see where we go as well."

Alex listened attentively, processing Maya's words. Her honesty struck a chord with him, and he appreciated her straightforwardness. He considered the delicate balance between their personal connection and the demands of their profession.

He was more than happy she brought the topic up. He had no way of knowing how to start that conversation himself.

"I appreciate your honesty, Maya," Alex responded a warm smile on his face. "I feel the same way. This job is crucial to both of us, and I respect that. Let's take it one step at a time and see where this journey leads us."

Maya's smile mirrored his own, a silent understanding passing between them. As they resumed their focus on the case, a newfound sense of camaraderie added another layer to their partnership, navigating the intricate terrain of both professional and personal realms.

Maya observed Alex rubbing his head and couldn't help but notice the strain on his face. Concerned, she inquired, "What's wrong, Alex?"

He sighed, then decided to share his recent experience. "I had a dream, Maya. I was walking in the cemetery where Henry was killed. It felt... haunting."

Maya nodded, understanding the toll the case was taking on him. "The stress is getting to you, isn't it?" she asked sympathetically.

"Yeah," Alex admitted. "It's just a lot to process."

Maya reassured him, "I get it. This case is taking a toll on all of us. Remember, I'm here if you need anything, even to talk."

"Thanks, Maya," Alex replied, appreciating the support. They both knew that navigating the complexities of the investigation, coupled with the personal challenges, required a strong support system. She gave him a look of appreciation. Afterward, they returned their attention to the task, determined to unravel the mysteries ahead.

Alex thanked Maya for her understanding and headed toward his office. As he settled in, his phone rang, and he noticed it was Nathan calling. Curious, he answered, "Hey, Nathan. What's going on?"

Nathan's voice sounded urgent. "Alex, you need to get to the coffee shop. I've got something that might be relevant to the case."

Intrigued, Alex replied, "I'm on my way." He quickly grabbed his jacket and left the police station, the anticipation building as he wondered what new development awaited him at the coffee shop.

As Alex approaches the coffee shop, he notices Nathan looking unusually serious outside. Nathan gestures for him to join, and as Alex approaches, Nathan shares the intriguing discovery.

"I got a call to collect information," Nathan starts, his voice carrying a mix of excitement and concern. "The owner told me that while reviewing the security camera footage from outside, he spotted a man on the day of the murder. That man walked towards the cemetery. What caught his attention later was seeing Henry taking the same path."

Alex and Nathan approach the owner inside the coffee shop, exchanging polite greetings. Alex gets straight to the point, asking, "Could you show us the footage you mentioned? We're curious to see what you found."

The owner nods and leads them to a small office where the security system is monitored at the back of the shop. As they gather around the computer, the owner starts playing the relevant footage from the day of the murder. The timestamp indicates it's the morning hours before the incident occurred. The three of them watch intently, observing the movements captured by the camera.

Alex leans in, scrutinizing the screen as the mysterious figure strolls by. The blue hoodie conceals the person's identity, and their face remains hidden in the shadows of the hood. Nathan glances at Alex, a sense of anticipation in the air. The footage continues, showing the man walking toward the cemetery.

"That's the same person from the museum," Alex remarks, a mix of curiosity and intensity in his voice. "But we still can't see who it is."

Nathan agrees, "It's a lead, though. Let's see if there's anything more." The footage progresses, capturing the man's movements. They continue watching, hoping for more clues to unravel the mystery.

Alex and Nathan exchange glances, perplexed by Henry's unexpected demeanor in the footage. The contrast between the mysterious figure and Henry's seemingly carefree walk raises more questions than answers.

"Did he know this person?" Nathan wonders aloud, his eyes fixed on the screen.

Alex leans back, deep in thought. "It's as if he was meeting someone, and it wasn't an antagonistic encounter."

Nathan nods in agreement. "Could they have been working together? Or was Henry simply excited about something?"

The duo continues to analyze the footage, attempting to decipher the connection between Henry and the person in the blue hoodie. The coffee shop buzzes with its usual activity, unaware of the pivotal clues on the screen.

Alex tells the owner to rewind to the suspect and freeze the video.

Alex stared intently at the frozen frame on the coffee shop's security footage. The enigmatic figure, draped in a blue hoodie, almost blended into the shadows. The hands nestled deep within the pockets, the face shrouded by the hood – it was an infuriatingly elusive identity.

Alex thanks the store owner for the video. He and Nathan leave the store, processing what they just saw.

As they stepped out into the crisp air, the atmosphere seemed charged with the possibilities of progress. Nathan looked at Alex and inquired, "So, where are you off to next?"

"I'm heading back to the cemetery," Alex replied. "Gonna try and trace the steps of our mysterious figure. Maybe find clues about who he is and where he went after the murder."

Nathan nodded in understanding. "Alright, man. Stay safe out there."

Alex offered a slight smile. "You too, Nathan.."

With that, they exchanged a few more parting words and went their separate ways. Nathan climbed into his car, and Alex headed back to the cemetery.

The cemetery lay silent and still as Alex approached the tree, the same one where the witness had seen the mysterious figure. However, as he drew closer, he noticed something that had eluded him. From a distance, it appeared as though someone had affixed an object to the tree—perhaps a piece of paper.

His curiosity piqued, and Alex quickened his pace until he stood before the tree. There, pinned to the rough bark, was a piece of paper.

The stark black letters carried a weight that seemed to shock the quiet cemetery, and the content struck a chilling chord in the detective's mind.

The words on the paper revealed a message, one that carried an ominous tone. It spoke of a belief that what had occurred, the unsettling events surrounding Henry's demise, was necessary for the greater good of Pineworth. The document hinted at the notion that Henry was on the brink of disrupting the established order, threatening the status quo that the writer seemed determined to preserve.

Was this an attempt to make a confession without being caught? Was the killer having doubts about why he killed Henry?

Or could this be a twisted manifesto for someone who really thinks he should be appreciated for doing what he did?

So many questions ran through his mind about the letter.

Alex's facial expression betrayed the unease that settled upon him as he absorbed the cryptic message. The mention of Henry's intentions and the writer's adamant stance that they had no alternative but to act sent shivers down his spine.

Alex retrieved a clear evidence bag from his kit. With gloved hands, he delicately peeled the letter off the tree and secured it within the protective confines of the bag. The crinkling of the plastic cut through the stillness of the cemetery, underscoring the eeriness.

As he sealed the evidence bag, Alex couldn't help but feel a weighty sense of responsibility. The letter held clues, perhaps the key to understanding the motives behind Henry's death and the broader implications for Pineworth. Determined, he made a mental note to analyze the contents of the message with meticulous care once he returned to the station.

With the evidence bag safely in hand, Alex took a final glance at the tree, contemplating the mysteries it had seen.

Alex took a deep breath before entering Chief Brown's office. The atmosphere seemed heavy with the weight of the ongoing investigation. Chief Brown looked up from his desk, his expression a mix of curiosity and concern.

"Chief, I've got something important to share," Alex began, holding a copy of the letter. "It was attached to the tree near where the witness saw the suspect at the cemetery."

Chief Brown's eyes narrowed as he took the letter from Alex. He carefully examined the typed message on the paper, absorbing the disturbing content.

Alex hesitated for a moment before relaying the chilling message. "It suggests that Henry's murder was committed to maintain the 'status quo' of Pineworth. The writer claims that Henry was going to disrupt things, leaving them no choice but to act."

Chief Brown's stern expression deepened into a frown. "This just got a lot more complicated. If someone is willing to kill to protect secrets, we're dealing with something bigger than a family feud."

Alex nodded, feeling the seriousness of the situation. "I've sent it for analysis, hoping we can find a fingerprint or any lead to the person behind this."

The Chief sighed. "Keep me posted, Alex. This might be the breakthrough we need to crack this case wide open."

With that, Alex left the chief's office, the unresolved mysteries of Pineworth weighing heavily on his shoulders. The journey to uncover the truth had taken an unexpected turn, and the shadow of danger seemed to loom larger than ever over the quiet town.

Alex walked into Maya's office, the door closing behind him. The faint murmur of office activity filled the room, but there was an air of tension shining through in the atmosphere.

Maya looked up from her desk, offering a congratulatory smile. "Nice work on finding that letter, Alex. It's a significant lead."

He sighed, running a hand through his hair. "It's like the killer wanted us to find it. Left it there for me to discover. Sending a message or trying to lead us in a certain direction."

Maya leaned forward, her eyes narrowing with a glint of determination. "Maybe the killer messed up and left some kind of evidence on that paper. We should have it analyzed thoroughly – fingerprints, DNA, anything that could give us a lead."

Alex nodded in agreement. "Exactly. I've already sent it for analysis. Let's hope it yields something substantial."

As the night wore on, the dim glow of the police station's fluorescent lights cast long shadows across the desks in Maya's office. The rhythmic tapping of keys rang out as Alex and Maya delved into the intricacies of the case, determined to decipher the enigma that shrouded Pineworth.

The air was heavy with the scent of coffee – the fuel that kept them alert during those relentless hours. The occasional drum of the printer and the distant whirring of a computer fan provided a backdrop to their focused collaboration. Fading into the background, the city slept while these two relentless minds refused to rest.

In the quiet camaraderie of the office, with only the soft glow of monitors illuminating their faces, Alex and Maya forged ahead. Clues were pieced together, theories were debated, and the urgency of the investigation fueled their determination.

As the first hints of dawn painted the sky outside, they pressed on, driven by a shared commitment to unravel the truth behind Henry's murder.

Despite being the lead detective, Alex found solace in Maya's unwavering commitment to the case. The collaborative atmosphere they created during those late-night sessions served as a catalyst for creative brainstorming and critical thinking. Maya's presence brought a sense of camaraderie, a partner in the pursuit of justice.

"You know Maya, I was always content doing this kind of stuff by myself." He offers.

"Yeah, you were quite known for that around here. I always thought that you were the best just because you were able to do everything alone. To be honest, I always read your reports to try to learn from you. You are very bright and know the law." She responds.

"Well, I guess I was always so proud. I wanted to be the best detective. Now, I am just now starting to see that being the best doesn't mean doing everything alone. Sometimes, it means being able to take a suggestion or advice. Or even view it from a second set of eyes." He says.

Alex continued, "Also, you know I have read all of your reports too. You have a great ability to include so many details in them. I have tried to emulate you in that regard."

They shared a mutual smile as they kept looking at the casework. Alex realized Maya had become someone he appreciated.

Alex appreciated Maya's dedication not only to the investigation but also to him. The weight of the case and the persistent shadows of Pineworth's secrets could be overwhelming. However, with Maya by his side, the intensity of the situation was tempered. Her insight and different perspective provided a fresh angle of approach, helping Alex to focus and consider aspects he might have overlooked.

As they worked side by side in the dimly lit office, coffee mugs and paperwork scattered across the desks, their collaborative efforts fueled a relentless pursuit of the truth.

The shared burden of responsibility became a bond that transcended professional obligations, fostering a connection that went beyond the surface of their roles.

In those late-night hours, Maya's dedication became a source of strength for Alex. Her decision to stay over and lend her expertise was not just an act of duty; it was a testament to their shared commitment to bringing justice to Pineworth.

Chapter 12
On The Campaign Trail

AS THE SUN BEGAN TO cast its early morning light through the office windows, Maya stood up, stretching her tired muscles. "I'm gonna head home to get a few hours of shut-eye," she said to Alex.

"Alright then, take care. I'll see you soon," Alex replied with a smile, looking up from his desk.

She turned to him with concern in her eyes. "What about you? What's your plan?"

"I'm going to swing by the mayoral debate at the town hall," Alex replied. "I want to meet this new candidate who seems to be shaking things up for the Carters."

Maya nodded understandingly. "Alright, just don't overwork yourself. Call me if you need anything."

"I will. Get some good rest," Alex said, offering a tired but appreciative smile.

Alex gathered his things as Maya left the office, preparing to face another day of mystery.

As Alex stepped out of the police department, he encountered Sarah entering for her day's work. Her eyes widened in surprise. "Oh my God, you've been here all night?" she asked, concern on her face.

He sighed, nodding. "Yeah, this case has me up at all hours. Have you taken Lizzy to school already?" he inquired.

Sarah nodded with an equally tired smile. "Yeah, she wasn't too happy about going until she saw James at the front of the school. Then all of a sudden, she was excited."

Alex chuckled. "James has that effect on people, I guess. Well, I better get going. Take care, Sarah."

"You too, Alex. And get some rest if you can," she advised as they parted ways.

Alex hopped into his car and made his way to the coffee shop. The jingle of the doorbell greeted him as he entered. The smell of freshly brewed coffee hit him. He knew that a good cup of coffee was exactly what he needed to keep him awake and alert.

He approached the counter and was greeted by the friendly owner. "The usual, Alex?" he asked with a smile.

"Absolutely," he replied, appreciating the comfort of routine, especially in the middle of a complex investigation. Waiting for his coffee, he glanced around the shop, waving at the regulars and feeling a sense of community that only a local coffee spot could provide.

With a warm cup in hand, he found a corner table. He settled in to review his notes and prepare for the day ahead. The gentle vibration of conversation and the soothing jazz music in the background created a conducive atmosphere for focus and relaxation.

As Alex sat at the corner table, gazing out of the window toward the cemetery, a wave of reflection washed over him. The view seemed to contain the energy of Henry's last moments, creating an unintentional connection between the detective and the victim.

The graveyard, shrouded in morning mist, stood silent and daunting. Headstones, like guardians of stories untold, stretched out across the landscape. Alex sipped his coffee, the warmth of the cup in his hands providing an obvious difference to the chill of the memories that hung in the air.

He found himself lost in thought, wondering about the mystery that surrounded Henry's death. The loud sounds of the coffee shop faded into the background, and he became one with the solitude of his own thoughts.

He wished Maya was there with him now, her company providing a soothing balm to the stress and uncertainty that surrounded the case. In a room filled with strangers, the absence of her familiar presence left a void that only she could fill. With a sigh, Alex took another sip of his coffee, the bitter taste reflecting the bitter reality of the investigation he found himself immersed in.

Alex leaves the coffee shop to walk around the town square.

As Alex wandered through the town square, the huge signs and hats endorsing the Carter campaign seemed to fill every inch of the busy storefronts. Store owners, eager to express their support for the incumbent mayor, prominently displayed campaign paraphernalia, creating a visual spectacle of the political landscape.

The windows of small boutiques proudly showcased the signature hats captured in the surveillance footage. Rows of them, neatly arranged and available for purchase, adorned the shelves like a symbol of unity within the community.

The signs were just as pervasive, acting as constant reminders of the impending mayoral election. Banners stretched across the streets, proclaiming "Carter for Mayor" in bold letters, and posters adorned the lampposts, adding a splash of color to the town's architecture. Even in the smaller mom-and-pop stores, one couldn't escape the visual campaign, as handmade signs proudly declared their endorsement for the incumbent.

Despite the busy atmosphere, Alex couldn't shake the feeling that beneath the civic engagement, there was a complex connection of hidden truths. The small town square, usually a symbol of community, now felt like a stage where political drama unfolded against the backdrop of an ongoing investigation. As he observed the abundance of signs and hats, he couldn't help but wonder if the answers to the darkness he sought were hidden in plain sight.

As Alex mused over the peculiarities of the campaign, a nagging question reiterated in his mind: Why would someone resort to murder if the election didn't pose any threat to the Carter family's political standing? The thriving support evident in the plethora of campaign materials and the absence of any visible competition for the opposing candidate fueled the detective's curiosity.

As he got back to his vehicle, Alex decided to go back to a place he hadn't been in a while.

As Alex parked his car near the gas station, a wave of memories from his days on patrol flooded back. He remembered seeing Marcus lying on the ground at this same location. The worn-out appearance of the place, perhaps even more dilapidated than before, struck a chord of nostalgia and somber reflection.

Amidst the faded hues of the gas station, a sign caught Alex's attention. It proudly displayed the name "Lorraine Jackson" as the candidate for mayor. Lorraine's determined face, accompanied by slogans promising change and community improvement, offered a stark contrast to the dominant presence of the Carter campaign in the town square.

Intrigued by the unexpected appearance of a formidable opponent, Alex pondered the dynamics at play. Lorraine Jackson seemed to embody a challenge to the longstanding reign of the Carter family. As he stared at the sign, a new set of questions unfolded in his mind, deepening the mystery of Henry's murder and the intricate connections between politics, power, and the hidden currents of Pineworth.

As Alex contemplated the implications of Lorraine Jackson's candidacy, he couldn't shake the feeling that she represented a voice for those who sought change, a departure from the entrenched influence of the founding families. Her focus on the people, distinct from the Carter-centric narrative, had the potential to resonate with a significant portion of the community.

As he pulls out of the gas station, he thinks of Marcus again. The image of the little boy will be forever in his mind.

He thought back to the funeral. Seeing the family there mourning. It was the first time he wanted to be on the case. Actually wanting to be there searching for the person that did this.

He noticed the time for the debate was getting close and started heading towards the town hall.

The atmosphere outside the town hall was charged with anticipation as a sizable crowd gathered, lending an air of importance to the upcoming mayoral debate. Alex noticed the diverse mix of people, their expressions reflecting curiosity, excitement, and perhaps a touch of tension. The significance of the occasion was palpable, and the energy in the air hinted at the potential impact the debate could have on the town's political landscape.

It seemed like the town was really showing up to see if someone is capable of standing toe to toe with Seth Cater.

As Alex parked his car and made his way toward the entrance, he couldn't help but have a sense of wonderment about the situation. The events unfolding around the mayoral campaign seemed to be reaching a critical juncture.

The pressure on him to uncover the truth intensified. The town hall, usually a place for community gatherings and events, now stood as the battleground for competing visions of Pineworth's future.

With each step, Alex braced himself for the revelations that might surface during the debate, wondering if the answers to the inescapable questions in his investigation would be unveiled in the political arena. The stakes were high, and the shadows of the past loomed large over the present, casting a complex and intricate web of connections that Alex sought to unravel.

The town hall buzzed with energy as the candidates were introduced, their names shooting through the room amid a mix of cheers and applause. Alex positioned himself near the front, slightly to the side, strategically choosing a vantage point that afforded him not only a clear view of the candidates and the debate but also an opportunity to gauge the reactions of the diverse crowd.

The room was an ocean of emotions, with supporters from both camps vocalizing their enthusiasm for their preferred candidate. Alex observed the distinct division within the crowd, reflecting the polarized sentiments that often accompanied political contests. The air crackled with anticipation as the candidates prepared to articulate their visions for Pineworth's future.

As the debate unfolded, each candidate presented their ideas, policies, and plans for the town.

The audience responded with varying degrees of enthusiasm, amplifying the charged atmosphere in the hall. Alex's focus alternated between the candidates' responses and the reactions of the onlookers, searching for any subtle cues or insights that might aid him in his ongoing investigation.

Alex's heart quickened as he scanned the crowd, disbelief washing over him. There, on the opposite side towards the back, a figure clad in a blue hoodie with the hood drawn and a hat obscuring their features was unmistakably making their way toward the front of the hall. The sight sent shivers down Alex's spine, a chilling realization dawning upon him – the elusive suspect from the footage had materialized right in the midst of the political event.

His detective instincts kicking into overdrive, Alex carefully maneuvered through the crowd, keeping a discreet distance as he tracked the mysterious figure's movements. The atmosphere in the hall, already charged with political tension, now carried an added layer of suspense as Alex trailed the potential suspect. He couldn't afford to lose sight of the individual who might hold the answers to the questions hovering over Pineworth.

As the hooded figure reached a few rows from the front, they lingered in the shadows, a silent observer of the unfolding debate. Alex's mind raced with questions, and he struggled to maintain composure. Was this a deliberate move by the suspect attending a high-profile event? Was it a bold attempt to stay one step ahead of the investigation or perhaps an audacious act of defiance?

The candidate's voices rolled through the hall, providing an unusual backdrop to the tension building within Alex. With each passing moment, the significance of the hooded figure's presence became more profound, casting a shadow over the proceedings. Alex knew he had to approach cautiously, threading the delicate line between maintaining order at a political event and unraveling the enigma that stood before him.

Adrenaline surged through Alex as he closed the gap between himself and the hooded suspect. With determination in his stride, he navigated through the crowd, intent on apprehending the elusive figure. But just as Alex reached the suspect, a sudden burst of speed signaled the start of a frantic pursuit.

Reacting swiftly, Alex keyed his radio, urgently broadcasting his pursuit to the police station. "This is Detective Harris. I'm in pursuit of a suspect on foot near the town hall. Blue hoodie, red hat, running towards the east side. Requesting backup."

The description rang over the police radio, and Alex continued to chase the suspect through the maze of streets surrounding the town hall. The suspect weaved through alleys and side streets, displaying an uncanny familiarity with the town's layout. Alex's determination matched the suspect's evasiveness, the pursuit intensifying with every turn.

As they darted through the dimly lit passages, the suspect's identity remained shrouded, the red hat bobbing in the distance.

Alex could hear the sirens coming close to his area. The radio rang out with requests for location updates.

As the chase continued, Alex noticed the man was running towards the cemetery. Sure enough, he did just that.

As the sun dipped below the horizon, casting the town in a twilight glow, Alex continued his pursuit through the cemetery. The words of the debate remained in the air, but the fading daylight added an eerie dimension to the chase. Tombstones stretched elongated shadows across the ground, creating an intricate web of darkness where the suspect could easily hide.

The length of the debate had prolonged the onset of night, leaving Pineworth in a state of transition between day and darkness. This in-between period, known as the "blue hour," painted the surroundings with deep blue hues, intensifying the pursuit's urgency.

The crackling of gravel beneath his shoes punctuated Alex's steps while he navigated the cemetery grounds. The changing landscape played tricks with shadows, making it increasingly challenging to discern reality from illusion. Shrouded in the dimming light, the suspect's silhouette blended seamlessly with the tombstones.

Alex's focus heightened as he moved cautiously through the rows of graves. The urgency of the chase was palpable, magnified by the fleeting twilight. The sun's departure marked a critical moment, demanding swift and precise action if he hoped to apprehend the suspect and unearth the answers hidden in the cemetery's historic grounds.

With urgency evident in every word, Alex's voice crackled over the radio. "Attention all units, we've got a suspect on foot. Blue hoodie, red hat. He's just entered the cemetery. I repeat, blue hoodie, red hat, in the cemetery. Secure all entrances, no one in or out until further notice."

The command reverberated through the airwaves, the importance of the situation hanging in the balance. Each word served as a directive, a call to action for every available officer to converge on the cemetery and ensure the suspect had no means of escape.

The radio went quiet, and the chase's intensity descended upon Alex. The cemetery, underneath the dimming twilight, was their current stage for this important point in the investigation.

Determined, Alex comprehended that their actions could get them nearer to the truth or let the suspect vanish into the darkness. Maya's footsteps echoed in the cemetery when she neared Alex, worry evident. "Did you get any information about the suspect's location?" she asked, her eyes scanning the dim light for any hint of movement.

Alex shook his head, frustration evident in his voice. "We're not sure. He was last seen running here, but I fear he got away. We've secured all entrances, but he vanished into thin air."

Maya mirrored his frustration, realizing the challenge they faced in the vast expanse of the cemetery. The setting sun created an eerie atmosphere as they grappled with the elusive suspect slipping through their fingers.

Nathan's voice crackled over the radio, "We've searched the whole cemetery, sir. No sign of the guy."

Alex sighed, disappointed in his response, "Alright, open the cemetery backup. Thanks for the effort, guys." The weight of the missed opportunity remained in the air as they realized the failure of the search.

Maya noticed the frustration etched on Alex's face as they walked back to his car together. Sensing his disappointment, she gently said, "You should get some rest, Alex. We'll regroup and figure out our next move."

Alex shook his head, still grappling that the suspect had slipped through his fingers. "I can't believe I let him get away," he muttered, the weight of the missed opportunity heavy on his shoulders.

Maya offered support, "You can't always catch the bad guy, Alex. But it's not over. You have a knack for finding the truth, and he won't get away in the long run."

Her reassurance brought some hope to Alex. They parted ways, each heading home to rest and prepare for the challenges ahead in the investigation.

Chapter 13
Memento Mori

WITH FATIGUE STILL lingering from the intense debate, Alex grudgingly lifts himself up from his bed. Despite the pressing weight of the unsolved case, determination strengthens his resolve as he realizes the need to propel forward and rekindle the investigation.

His mind is overwhelmed with thoughts of the elusive suspect in the blue hoodie as he prepares for the day. The unsuccessful pursuit at the cemetery plagues him, yet Alex remains resolute in his determination to overturn the situation and apprehend the offender.

He heads to the police station, ready to regroup. The testing of his mettle and the pursuit of the unknown continue, urging him forward into the heart of the investigation.

Chief Brown summons Alex into his office, a departure from their usual case-focused discussions. Once inside, Brown skips the customary case updates and asks a more personal question, catching Alex off guard.

"Alex," starts Chief Brown, "how's it hanging? This job's tough, and it's vital to check up on each other. You okay?" Caught off guard by his question, Alex pauses to acknowledge his kindness.

"You know, Chief," he answers, "It's rough. The case, it's tricky, it's draining me, but I'm keeping up. It's rare anyone cares to ask how I'm doing amidst all this craziness."

Chief Brown nods, emphasizing the importance of knowing the personal aspects of their demanding profession.

As they delve into a more intimate discussion, Alex finds solace in the unexpected empathy from his superior.

Chief Brown leans back in his chair, offering a piece of wisdom to Alex, "I know the chase didn't go as planned, but there's a saying I've always appreciated throughout history. Memento Mori."

Intrigued, Alex queries, "What does that mean?"

Chief Brown smiles knowingly, "It means 'remember you are mortal.' I see it as a reminder that we all have our limits and our moments of weakness. The pursuit of justice can be relentless, but it's essential to recognize our humanity in the process."

Alex takes a moment to absorb the wisdom, appreciating the perspective Chief Brown is sharing. The weight of the case and the recent events seem to momentarily lighten as the chief imparts a timeless truth.

Alex, with a nod of gratitude, tells the chief, "Sir, I've always gotten wisdom from your guidance throughout my career. And it's not just me; many others have mentioned similar sentiments. Where does all this wisdom come from?"

Chief Brown folded his arms, his gaze carrying the weight of countless years spent in the field. "Experience, Alex. It stems from setbacks, learning from them, and realizing that every stumbling block is a chance to evolve."

"Wisdom isn't merely grasping the 'what to do'; it's comprehending the 'why you do it,'" he added.

Alex absorbs the words, recognizing the invaluable lessons from the chief's experiences.

Chief Brown returns the conversation to the ongoing investigation, "Now, about the case. Do you feel like you're closing in on the suspect?"

Alex leaned forward, his eyes focused and determined. "Chief, the recent developments, the letter found at the cemetery, and now this suspect – it all seems to point in the same direction.

His escape, outfit, and tie to the mayor's race are like puzzle pieces fitting together. Something bigger than just avoiding capture is at play. I believe it's related to what Henry found. I'm not 100% sure, but I sense we're nearing the truth. We must persist."

Chief Brown agreed, "Memento Mori, Alex. Don't forget that seeking truth involves trials, and we should anticipate hiccups. It's our reactions to these hiccups that carve our characters. Stay goal-oriented, and don't let frustration cloud your thinking. Our community is depending on us to provide explanations."

Alex appreciated Chief Brown's words. "Thank you, Chief. I won't let this case go unsolved. We owe it to Henry, to his family, and the people of Pineworth."

The chief gave him a reassuring smile, "Good. Now, get back out there and continue the investigation. And remember, you're not alone in this – we're a team."

Alex left Chief Brown's office with a renewed sense of self. He had an eagerness to continue the case.

Entering his office, Alex found Maya unexpectedly there. He felt at ease with Maya around. Her help was valuable to him. Grinning, he said, "What's up, Maya?"

Maya returned the smile, "Just checking in on you. After everything with the suspect last night, I wanted to make sure you're doing okay."

"Thanks for that," Alex expressed, settling into his chair behind the desk. "It's been quite a ride, but I'm in a better place now."

Maya leaned forward, her expression carrying a mix of anticipation and curiosity. "I might have some good news," she said, handing Alex an envelope. "The results from the analysis on the letter came in."

Alex took the envelope and carefully opened it, revealing the contents inside. He quickly scanned the document, his eyes narrowing in focus. "And?" he prompted, eager to hear the outcome.

"Alex, I'm sorry, the letter didn't yield any evidence," Maya informed him, her tone reflecting the disappointment shared by both detectives. The lack of fingerprints or any identifiable traces on the letter added another layer of challenge to an already complex investigation.

Alex took a deep breath, absorbing the shock. The elusive killer seemed to leave behind no tangible leads, making the pursuit even more challenging. Despite the setback, the determination in their eyes remained, ready to explore new avenues and uncover the truth.

"Well, now I am not sure where to go from here," Alex says after a deep exhale.

"I really need to get something on this guy." he continues.

"Well, hopefully, he makes a mistake," Maya responds.

Alex vocalizes his concern about whether the suspect would strike again. He notes that the way the person approached the stage during the debate had an ominous and unsettling vibe.

Just at that moment, Alex received a call from Samantha.

"Samantha, hi, how can I help you?"

"Hey, Alex, you need to see this," Samantha continued. "It's an email from Henry talking about meeting the suspect at the cemetery. This could be a breakthrough!"

"Check your email; it was buried in my spam folder," Samantha exclaimed.

Perplexed, Alex quickly opened his email, searching for the forwarded message. As the subject line caught his eye, he realized its significance – it was from Henry, sent just before the murder.

Alex's mind raced as he absorbed the contents of the email. The mention of a meeting at the cemetery added a new layer to the investigation, providing a potential link between Henry and the suspect. Samantha's discovery had the potential to reshape the entire case, shedding light on a hidden aspect that could lead them closer to the truth.

Alex shows Maya the email.

"Looks like he forwarded an email sent by the killer. Details about meeting at the cemetery." Alex says.

"What is the address that was used?" Maya asks.

"Looks like a stonemaster30528@pnwork.com," He replies.

Alex looks at Maya. Both silently acknowledged the number 30528 as the zip code for Pineworth, Georgia.

"Thank you, Samantha. We will be in touch." Alex continues. He hangs up the phone and looks at Maya.

"This could be huge. You are more of a tech person than me. Can this be traced?" He asks her.

"Well, every email has the IP address information attached. If we can get a warrant to search that IP address, we could get a location from where it was sent."

"Awesome! I'll put that together now. This may be the only mistake this guy has made. We have to take advantage." Alex says somewhat excitedly.

After completing the necessary paperwork, Alex rushes to the courthouse to speak with Judge Phillips.

"Good morning, Detective Bennett. What brings you here this morning?" the judge asks.

"Well, sir, it is about the Winters case. I need to present a case for a warrant to be signed. I was given a forwarded email by the victim's sister. We need to get a warrant to trace the IP address to the location it was sent from. We hope that it will lead us to the suspect." Alex pleads.

Judge Phillips responds, "It sounds to me you have enough probable cause here to believe that the person behind this email was involved in Henry Winters's death. You have your warrant. Good luck, Detective."

Alex had a feeling of joy as he left the courtroom. He felt like he had not been this close to catching the suspect ever since the case started.

After getting the warrant signed, he rushed back to Maya.

"Got it signed!" he exclaimed.

"Okay, I will work on getting you that location," she says.

"Thank you, Maya. I know you also have your own cases you are working on. I appreciate all the help recently." he tells her.

"You know it's all good. We are a team here. It is important to get this thing solved." she replied.

Leaving Maya, Alex then went back to his office to think about what other leads to follow.

While sitting at his desk, he mapped out the whole case in his head.

He couldn't help but feel like he was closing in. Maybe that is why the suspect put the letter on the tree, to begin with. Did he realize his mistake in sending the email? Did he think that information was already known?

"Does this case come down to hoping he sent the email from a place we can connect the suspect to?' he thinks out loud.

Alex decides to go to grab some coffee for him and Maya. It was the least he could do for all the work she had done to help him with the case.

While walking from his car to the coffee shop, he once again sees the "Vote for Carter" hats at a store just beside the coffee shop.

Curious, he decides to walk into the store.

"Hi, come on in. If there is anything I can do, let me know." the female store worker says while putting a shirt on a hanger.

"Thank you," he said. "I actually was coming to look at some hats," Alex responds.

"Well, the Carter hats are flying off the shelf. Ever since we got them shipped in a few days ago." she chimes back.

Alex thinks again about his timeline. Then it hits him. "A few days ago? Do you know how long, to be exact?"

The woman stops making her shirts and says, "I got them four days ago, just a few days before the debate. I believe we were the first store to receive our order. They were a huge hit."

Alex thanks the woman and stands outside the store. He thinks to himself if the hats that the suspect was wearing were not being sold until after the day of the murder, then he had to be someone who had access to the hats when they were being made.

After grabbing coffee, Alex rushed back to the police department.

"I got you a coffee and some news!" he tells Maya, who is in her office.

"Well, as always, coffee first." she recipes.

Alex gives her the coffee and tells her the revelation about the hat.

She replies, "Well, that has to help. I have some news as well. We have a location in which the email was sent from."

Alex sits up straight, eager to hear. He nods at her and waves his hands towards himself to say tell me.

"1189 Oakdale Drive, Pineworth, Georgia," Maya says optimistically.

"No. It can't be." Alex says almost in a whisper.

Alex immediately grabs his phone and starts dialing.

"What is it? Do you know the address?" Maya asks.

Alex waits to respond. He dials the number, and when someone picks up, he says, "Hey, Mayor Carter, I am sorry to disturb you. Can you tell me who designed your hats?"

Alex waited for the answer. The time between asking the question and the answer seemed to last a lifetime.

"Yeah, sure, Detective, that would be my campaign manager and brother, Michael. So you like those hats?" the Mayor says in a proud voice.

"Yes, very much, Mayor. Do you know where Michael is now?" Alex inquired.

"Yeah, he is more likely than not to be at city hall. I gave him an office there while the campaign was ongoing. And just like him, it had to overlook the cemetery. You know him, ever the historian." Mayor Carter declares.

"Well, thank you, Mayor Carter. I don't want to take up any more of your time. See you around."

Alex then hangs up the phone.

He looks at Maya in disbelief.

"We got him. "

Chapter 14
A Chance at Justice

THE LIGHT FROM OUTSIDE barely made its way into Chief Brown's office. The space had become the place Alex had called a department meeting. He knew that everyone would be needed in the apprehension of the subject.

"So," Alex began, "I have called you all here because I will need all the help I can get to apprehend the suspect."

"So you know who the suspect is?" Chief Brown questioned.

Alex took a deep breath. He knew once he said who it was, everyone would doubt it. Seth had been in this town his whole life. As the brother of the Mayor, he had made friends with almost everyone. He even came off as a very joyful person to Alex himself.

"Yes, sir, I do," Alex replied. "It's Michael Carter."

A collective gasp was heard all over the room. Everyone had a shocked look on their face. Including Cheif Brown, who spoke and said, "Okay, listen up. We have a job to do here. I know most of you'll know Seth. Detective Bennett here will not say this without doing his homework first. So let us listen to what he has to say."

Alex then went over the details. The mood in the room changed with every detail. The faces went from surprise to disgust.

"We have a guy that has killed," Alex says to the group. "Also, a guy that ran from us not too long ago. We have to have the building surrounded. Be on the lookout. We don't know what he can do with his back against the wall."

Sgt. Harris announces that he and his men will be on the square to assist.

"Very good. Now I need someone to go into city hall to see if he is in his office. If I go in there, it might spook him into running again." Alex stated.

"I'll do it," replies Nathan.

"Okay, great," says Alex. "I will meet everyone on the town square in ten minutes."

After the meeting concluded, Chief Brown approached Alex and said good job conveying his message.

"You did well in there. Now go get this guy and put an end to this chase."

Alex responds, "Yes, sir."

Alex and Maya rode to the town square together. They parked at the coffee shop and looked at City Hall. They watched as police vehicles parked around the square. It was almost time.

"I hope this goes well," says Alex.

"It will. You have put in all the work," replied Maya.

The day of justice was finally here for Henry. It was a day that Alex was never quite sure would ever get here. Now, all he had to do was get his man.

The time to go had arrived as Nathan pulled up to city hall. Alex watched as he got out of the vehicle and entered the front of the building.

As they waited for the word to come that the suspect was inside, Alex turned to Maya. "you know I couldn't have done this without you."

Maya smiles and replies, "Oh, you would have gotten here without me. You truly are a great detective."

Alex smiles back. "Well, not just your help at work, but also the way you helped me outside of work. You have made me hopeful for a life I had given up on."

The conversation was cut short as they saw Nathan walk out of the building. The radio cracked with his voice, "All units, be advised the subject is in the building. Location top floor, back right room overlooking the cemetery."

Alex grabbed his radio and responded back, "All clear, all units just as planned. Detective Maya and I will enter and apprehend. Block all exits. No one in or out until we walk out with the subject."

As Alex and Maya walked into the towering halls of City Hall, the old building had an air of authority. The receptionist, a slight figure seated behind an old and heavy desk, looked up and greeted them with a warm, professional smile.

"Good morning," the receptionist said, her tone a careful balance between warmth and formality. "How can I assist you today?"

Alex, with a subtle nod, acknowledged the greeting. "We're here to see Michael Carter. It's regarding an ongoing investigation."

The receptionist advised. "Of course, Detective. Let me inform him of your arrival. Please have a seat; I'll make sure he'll be with you shortly."

Alex responds that it would be better if they showed themselves at his office.

The receptionist, catching onto the weight of the situation, nodded in agreement.

A tightness filled the air as the two detectives approached the top floor of the building. As they approached the office, typing could be heard coming from the room.

Alex approached the doorway. "Working on an email Michael?"

Michael looks up from his computer with a smile. "Detectives, welcome, come on in." He rises from his desk to gesture them in. "I didn't know ya'll would be coming up here."

"Michael, I am going to cut to the chase. Where were you the night of Henry Winters murder?" Alex questions in a firm voice.

Michael responds quickly, "At home, I'm sure. What is this about, friend?"

"It's about you being the one that killed Henry," Alex says bluntly.

After this statement, an obvious change was seen in Michael's usually happy face. "Look, Detective, I have told you I was at home that night, so if you don't have any evidence, I'm gonna have to ask you to leave."

"Here's the deal, we have evidence. We have the email, the torn clothing when you stole the gavel, the location you sent the email from, which is your home address, and a partial fingerprint, which I bet matches yours." Alex explains.

"What you have is assumptions," Michael says in a louder tone.

"No, what we have is a murderer who killed someone in cold blood for nothing!" Alex says, pressing into the suspects' consciousness.

Alex continued. "You sent an email to Henry saying you were with the Pineworth Chronicles. He met you there to expose you and your family. You just couldn't take the embarrassment."

A look of irritation and frustration washed over the killer. He began to breathe a little heavier. "You know nothing! I killed Henry because he was going to send his journal to a reporter. The page he claimed would cause the most harm was that my family kicked out people from this land that were already here."

"So you killed him for wanting to tell the truth?" Alex retorted.

"He was going to ruin not only my family legacy but many others. I wasn't the only one that was mad at him. I was just the only one that would stand up and defend us."

His tone became even more sinister than before.

"I am glad I did what I did. The gavel which was used by our ancestor, the first judge, was just a symbolic touch."

Alex paused before responding. "And the letter?"

"Oh, that was just a little explanation of why," Michael said with an evil smile.

"Well, I believe we have heard enough. Michael Carter, you are under arrest for the murder of Henry Winters." Alex says in a finished voice.

Alex and Maya escorted the now-arrested Michael out of the building and put him in the back of Nathan's patrol car.

A sense of finality came over him. A relief that felt like the weight of the world was lifted off of him.

As Nathan drove off with Seth, Alex stood and looked around. The Mayor was talking with Chief Brown. It looked like a heartfelt conversation. Obviously, he had been unaware as to what his brother was up to due to the look on his face.

Alex got back to the station to finish up the paperwork when James walked in.

"Hey man, congratulations on cracking the case. Never had any doubt." He says.

"Yeah, well, that makes one of us," Alex says with a chuckle. "I had a ton of help from everyone on this one."

"Hey, it is like that sometimes," James's demeanor shifts to a more calming tone, "You know that we all had faith in you."

Alex felt a warmth swell inside him. "I appreciate that," he says, "I really couldn't have done any of this without you asking me to come over or Maya helping me with everything."

"Speaking of Detective Sinclair, you two seemed to be hitting it off last time I saw ya'll hanging out. Don't deny it. I am good at this stuff." James quips.

"I think we are going to see where this relationship takes us. We both have a hole that needs to be filled in our lives," Alex leans back in his chair, "And thanks to your invite, I believe we are even closer now than we could've ever thought."

James puts his hand over his chest. "Well, I am just saving the world, one person at a time. Don't mind me."

James and Alex go over the events that lead to the arrest of Michael Carter. "I would have never guessed! I grew up with him. Always seemed like a stand-up guy." James exclaims.

"Well, I guess we all have a little bit about us that no one ever really knows about," Alex responds.

The conversation comes to a close with a friendly goodbye. Alex finished up his paperwork and made his way to his car to pay the Winter family a visit. He wanted to be the one to update them on the case.

Driving to the Winters home was bittersweet. On one hand, you had the news that the killer had been apprehended. On the other, you still had a grieving family that is missing such a great husband and father.

The trip out to the Winters home was calm. For the first time in a long time, his phone never rang. It was like the universe was rewarding him for the work he had put into solving the case.

While driving, he thought about all the times his own father would take him on car rides around the town and its outskirts.

He remembered his father telling him. "That right there is the Winters home. They are good people. Not only are they one of the families that founded this place, but they do all they can for the people here in this town."

It was shocking to him that this memory had not come up before this drive. All the late nights he spent working on this case, and it never showed up.

Getting closer to the house, Alex sees a large eagle flying from tree to tree. Was it just an ordinary bird, or perhaps the spirit of Henry coming to say thank you.

Alex got to the home and found both Mrs. Winters and Matthew outside, sitting on the porch.

"Hello, I am sorry to intrude. I wanted to come and update you both in person on the case." He takes a moment to make sure he says the right thing. "We have arrested Michael Carter for the murder of Henry."

He could tell there was a relief washing over both mother and son. It was the news that they had been waiting for.

Mrs. Winters looks up to the sky in appreciation. "Thank you, Detective, for everything you have done. Not only catching the man who did this but coming here yourself to give us the news. We appreciate all the hard work you have put into this."

"Yes, ma'am," he starts, "I know it isn't over for ya'll. There will be court dates and a lot more. I hope this news brings a little bit of comfort."

"Matthew," he continued, "Your father was a great man. The things he did, as well as the things he was trying to do, were for the better of the people of this town. Be proud. You carry a legacy with you. If you ever need anything, just let me know. I will do anything I can to help."

Matthew just shakes his head in acknowledgment.

Alex had hoped to tell Matthew something to be proud of his father for. He could tell by his silent response that he had done that.

The conversation comes to an end as Alex tells the family goodbye. He felt pride in himself and his profession. To be able to bring some sort of peace to a family in need is why he went into law enforcement, to begin with.

Before getting into his car, he receives a text message from Maya reading, "Coffee shop?".

Of course, he jumped at the opportunity.

On the way to meet Maya, he drives slowly. Taking in the nature around him. Who knows when he will be able to just drive and enjoy his day. There will always be another day, another case. But for now, all he had to think about was her.

When he arrived at the shop, he could tell Maya had a nonprofessional expression on her face. He could get to know her more with the case no longer in his mind.

"So, how did the family take the news?" she asked.

"They were appreciative. I think they are still grieving, which is to be expected. Hopefully this helps." He replies.

"You have actually made a difference in someone else's life, Alex. I hope you understand that," she says.

"Well, I hope so. They deserve all they can get after something like that happens to them." He replied.

As they sat and talked, Alex thought about the course his life had taken due to the case. He had come closer to friends like James, Nathan, and Maya. He had learned more about what people think of him and his work ability. It felt good to have the support he had been given throughout.

After finishing their coffee, Alex asks if Maya could walk with him through the cemetery.

Passing through the gates felt different than before as if the aura that had once been there was lifted. "This was the place of my nightmares," He tells her, "Now it feels so different coming in here,"

Maya responds. "You are a big reason why it feels different."

"Do you think, years from now, that people will remember what happened to Henry here at this spot?" Alex asks.

After taking a moment, she responded, "I think people will remember what he stood for. He was a man with morals, one that was sick of the status quo, and that sticks in the minds of people."

"Good," Alex thought out loud. The thought of Henry not being remembered upset him. He saw something in himself that related to the struggle that Henry went through. There is a need to get answers and expose them to the masses.

Perhaps the case he solved wasn't just a murder. It was also a story of a town that is in need of a new way of thinking.

All the long nights on the beat had shown Alex the difference in the lives of people in the town. Some are comfortable, others not. Hopefully, with his help, Henry got his message out to the world. A message that would transform how the town could change for the better.

Leaving the cemetery, Alex acknowledged the ending of the case in himself. For him, it was closed forever. A giant footnote in not only his career but a big part of Pineworth's history.

As they got back to the main road, Maya turned to Alex and asked, "Walk me home?"

Alex smiled and replied, "Yeah, of course, someone has to save the bad guys from you."

As they walked away, Maya took his hand. The daylight was beginning to fall. The sun casting imperfect waves of light blocked only by the streaks of clouds that dare come between it and the earth below.

The quiet town of Pineworth was winding down. Who knows what mystery awaited?

Epilogue

Pineworth would eventually heal from the wounds that Seth Carter caused. The town museum was renamed the Henry Winters Museum.

New Mayor Lorraine Jackson became the first non-Carter to lead the city into new territories.

Detective Bennett found a resolution in the closed case. He fostered meaningful relationships both in his field of work and in his personal life. At least once a week, he stops by the grave of Henry Winters. Reminding him that there will always be those who try to stop the ones that do the right thing.

As the days went by after the case, the town moved forward. They learned to always look in the shadows. Pineworth's street shined with resilience as the community determined to rebuild. It redefined itself and went beyond the dark secrets of the past.

The Pineworth Chronicle wrote an article referencing the journal Henry held most dear. The piece sent off a chain reaction and the downfall of a once powerful family, and the residents, although scared, came away with newfound strength.

James still held a weekly cookout at his house. The group that attends gets closer and closer as friends.

Mrs. Winters now fills her time working at the museum. The journal that was once held in her late husband's hands now sits behind a display where you can get a firsthand account of who Henry Winters was as a person.

Sarah and Nathan now share a last name. Her daughter is ever so happy to have him in her life.

The epilogue of this story marks not only the end of a monopolized society in the city but also the start of a new way of life. One that once held its secrets among the stones.

Don't miss out!

Visit the website below and you can sign up to receive emails whenever K.E.W. publishes a new book. There's no charge and no obligation.

https://books2read.com/r/B-A-RJUBB-NUCWC

BOOKS 2 READ

Connecting independent readers to independent writers.

Did you love *Secrets Among The Stones*? Then you should read *The Pineworth Chronicles*[1] by K.E.W.!

"The Pineworth Chronicles," a compelling series that delves into the challenges and sacrifices faced by first responders. In this gripping collection, readers will be immersed in the demanding world of emergency services, gaining a profound understanding of the trials and triumphs these heroes encounter.Book 1: "The Crossroads of Duty" explores the complex decisions that first responders confront in critical moments. Join our protagonists as they navigate the ethical dilemmas that arise when duty clashes with personal beliefs, witnessing the profound impact these choices have on their lives and the lives of those they serve.Book 2: "The Often Forgotten Hero" shines a light on the unsung heroes of emergency services. Dive into the stories of

---

1. https://books2read.com/u/m26K2o

2. https://books2read.com/u/m26K2o

individuals who tirelessly work behind the scenes, providing crucial support and expertise. Discover the immense contributions made by these often overlooked figures and develop a newfound appreciation for their indispensable role in the first responder community.Book 3: "The Rookie's Journey" takes readers on an emotional rollercoaster as we follow a young and inexperienced first responder. Witness their transformation from a wide-eyed novice to a seasoned professional, as they navigate the intense physical and emotional challenges that come with the job. Experience their growth, resilience, and self-discovery throughout their journey.

Also by K.E.W.

The Pineworth Chronicles
The Crossroads Of Duty
The Often Forgotten Hero
A Rookie's Journey
Secrets Among The Stones

Standalone
The Pineworth Chronicles

About the Author

K.E.W. is the pseudonymous voice behind a budding literary journey, merging the worlds of law enforcement and storytelling. Having served within law enforcement since 2016, and as a deticated school resource officer from 2021, K.E.W. draws inspiration from these experiences.Through their writing, K.E.W. seeks to illuminate the intricate struggles inherent in upholding the law whilechampioning social justice reform. Their poignant narratives delve into these complexities, aiming to resonate particularly with the young minds frequenting the hallways of local public schools. K.E.W.'s debut works offer thought-provoking insights and inspiring tales woven from the fabric of their unique career path.

About the Publisher

White Quill Writings was founded in 2023 on the shared passion for storytelling and literary expression, White Quill Writings is the brainchild of a devoted husband and wife duo. With a vision to empower authors and bring exceptional stories to life, they embarked on this self-publishing venture.

Driven by a commitment to support emerging voices and diverse narratives, White Quill Writings offers a platform that values creativity, authenticity, and individuality. Their dedication to nurturing writers shines through personalized guidance, professional editing, and tailored publishing solutions.

As a testament to their unwavering belief in the power of words, this partnership fosters a community where stories flourish, authors thrive, and dreams of publication become tangible realities. White Quill Writings stands as an inviting gateway for writers seeking to share their unique tales with the world.

Read more at https://instagram.com/whitequillwritings.